Fairy Tales
FOR YOUNG READERS

LIVE UNITED

United Way
of Jackson County

This Book Donated By:

INTERNET
ESSENTIALS
from Comcast

Fairy Tales
FOR YOUNG READERS

BY THE AUTHOR OF
SHAKESPEARE'S STORIES FOR YOUNG READERS
E. NESBIT

DOVER PUBLICATIONS, INC.
MINEOLA, NEW YORK

Bibliographical Note

Fairy Tales for Young Readers: By the Author of Shakespeare's Stories for Young Readers, first published by Dover Publications, Inc., in 2015, is a newly reset, unabridged republication of the work originally published as *The Old Nursery Stories* by Henry Froude and Hodder and Stoughton, London, in 1908. The original illustrations have been omitted from this edition.

Library of Congress Cataloging-in-Publication Data

Nesbit, E. (Edith), 1858–1924.
    [Old nursery stories.]
    Fairy tales for young readers : by the author of Shakespeare's stories for young readers / E. Nesbit.
        p. cm.
    "A newly reset, unabridged republication of the work originally published as The Old Nursery Stories by Henry Froude and Hodder and Stoughton, London, in 1908. The original illustrations have been omitted from this edition."
    Summary: A collection of nine fairy tales retold, including such favorites as Cinderella and Puss in Boots, as well as the less familiar stories of Dick Whittington and His Cat and Hop-o'-my-Thumb.
    Includes bibliographical references and index.
    ISBN-13: 978-0-486-78940-8 (pbk.)
    ISBN-10: 0-486-78940-3 (pbk.)
    1. Fairy tales. [1. Fairy tales.] I. Title.

PZ8.B612OI5 2015
398.2—dc23
[E]   2014036054

Manufactured in the United States by Courier Corporation
78940301   2015
www.doverpublications.com

Contents

Fairy Tales

FOR YOUNG READERS

CINDERELLA

THERE WAS ONCE a gentleman of a fine fortune and studious habits who had a dear wife and one little daughter. And all three were so fond of each other that there were not three happier people in the world. The little daughter grew up very beautiful, very good, and quite clever enough to be the light of her parents' eyes. And when she was fifteen Bad Fortune, which seemed to have forgotten this happy little family, suddenly remembered them. The mother caught a fever and died in three days. The father was heartbroken. He would not leave the house even to walk in the pleasant gardens that lay round it. He would not even open one of his once-loved books, and it was difficult to get him to eat enough to keep the life in him. He would sit, all day long, looking at the chair where his wife had been used to sit with her book or her sewing. His daughter tried in vain to rouse him, and at last she began to be afraid that if he went on like this he would lose his reason.

So she persuaded him to give away his house and furniture to his poor neighbours, and to go a long journey to a distant country, where there would be nothing to remind him of the dear treasure he had lost.

Arrived in the new country, he did indeed seem less wretched. He became once more absorbed in his studies, but he ate and drank what was set before him, and did not refuse to go out for walks, or sometimes to a neighbour's house to supper. But he was a changed and broken man to the day of his death.

He had a kind and gentle nature, and he imagined that all women were as good as his dear dead wife, so that when a neighbour told him that a certain widow lady was dying of love for him the simple gentleman said, "If this be so I will marry her—only she must be told that my heart is buried in my wife's grave."

"She will bear with that," said the match-making neighbour, "and her two girls will be nice company for your daughter."

So the widow married the gentleman, and that was the beginning of trouble. Because it was not he that she loved, but his fortune—and as for his daughter, she and her girls hated the poor child from the first, though they pretended to be very fond of her until everything was settled as they wished.

Directly after the wedding he said to his new wife:

"My dear, we are now married, which is what you wanted. All that I have is yours, and you are the mistress of my house. Be kind to my poor child, and please arrange everything without bothering me. My books are my constant companions, and you may entertain your friends as much as you like as long as you leave me in peace."

In this way he handed over his daughter to her stepmother and step-sisters.

Now as soon as these saw that the master of the house never noticed anything that went on in it, and that his daughter was much too fond of her father to worry him with complaints, they decided to put that child in her proper place. They began by forbidding her to appear at table when there was company. Then they said she might as well make herself useful and dust her own and her sisters' rooms. Then she was told to sweep as well as dust. After that the washing of the dishes was put upon her. And soon she was doing the work of a housemaid, a parlour-maid, a kitchen-maid, two general servants, and a boy in buttons, without a penny of wages or a kind word from month's end to month's end. All her jewels and pretty clothes were taken away—the jewels her father had bought for her, and the clothes sewn and embroidered for her by the loving hands of her dead mother. She used to sit on the kitchen hearth and cry when the servants had gone to bed, to think of the happy times when her mother was alive and her father had not grown stupid and helpless with sorrow. And as she sat crying one day Marigolda, the eldest sister, came rustling into the kitchen in her pink flounced silk, and saw her among the ashes, and laughed and said:

"Don't put the fire out with all those water fountains, you nasty, dirty little Cinderella!"

And after that she was never called anything else. And she was called all day long. It was, "Cinderella, you haven't made my bed," "Cinderella, black my boots this minute," "Cinderella, mend my lace collar," "Cinderella, peel the potatoes," "Cinderella, clean the kitchen grate," and a thousand other "Cinderellas," each with some work tacked on to it, from morning till night.

Cinderella did her best. But it is difficult to be in half a dozen places at once—which was the least that her step-relations expected of her. She would not complain to her father. She was determined to bear everything rather than make him unhappy.

She had only the commonest clothes to wear, and even they were ragged, because she had no time to mend them. She ate the least pleasant bits left over from yesterday's dinner, and her bed was a wooden box full of straw in a corner of the kitchen, which she shared with the kitchen cat and the fat old turnspit dog, who were her only friends.

"Oh, well," sighed poor Cinderella, "I must just go on bearing it, and if I am good something nice will happen to me some day."

And sure enough something did.

The King of that country had his palace quite near the house where Cinderella lived so uncomfortably. And the

King's son happening to be twenty-one, the King decided to give birthday parties every night until he should have invited all the gentlepeople who lived near. Father and mother and Dressalinda and Marigolda were invited, but the gentleman who arranged the invitations had never heard of Cinderella, who had not a single friend in that strange country to speak a word for her when the cards were being sent out.

Dressalinda and Marigolda were immensely excited when the invitation came, brought by a herald blowing a trumpet and walking very stately, with a train of beef-eaters bearing hundreds of large gilded envelopes with crowns on the flaps, in silver waste-paper baskets. And when the girls tore open the envelope and saw the gilded card with the royal arms on it, and their own names, they were wild with delight, because everybody knew that this series of birthday parties was given so that the young prince might see as many girls as possible, and that out of them all he might choose a bride. He was such a very nice young man, to say nothing of his being the Prince and the heir to all the kingdom, that no one imagined that any girl could say anything but "Yes" if he should say, "Will you marry me?"

And no girl could have said it unless she had happened to be in love with some other nice young man.

And now nothing was talked of but the royal ball. Cinderella had to do her dirty kitchen work just as usual, and besides that she had to wash and iron every petticoat and chemisette, every scrap of lace or muslin that her step-sisters had—to mend and iron all their fine dresses, because they had decided to try on every single thing they had, so as to see what suited them best. I should have thought they might have got new dresses and have done with it. But they didn't. Perhaps it was because no money could have bought them the delicate gold and coloured embroidery, the fairy-like lace that Cinderella's mother had wrought and woven for her dear little daughter.

The great day came at last, and father, step-mother, and step-sisters went off in the family coach. The last words Cinderella heard were:

"Now, you lazy little cat, be sure to tidy up our rooms before you dare to go to bed."

So she sighed as the wheels of the coach rumbled away, and set herself to do as she was told, and tidy up the litter of laces, ribbons, hair-pins, curl-papers, slippers, dressing-gowns, artificial flowers, fans, brooches, necklaces, handkerchiefs, bracelets, veils, tiaras, and all the rest of it. And when that was done she sat down in the quiet kitchen among the grey ashes, and cried and cried and cried.

"Oh, I wish," she sobbed out at last, "oh, I *do* wish I could go to the ball!"

"Do you, love? Then you shall!" said a voice quite close to her—such a kind voice too; and it was more than a year since she had heard a voice that was kind.

She started up, and found herself face to face with a fairy. She knew at once that it was a fairy, though the face was gentle enough to have been an angel's, because the wings were fairy-shape, and not angel-shape.

"Oh!" she cried, "who are you?"

"I'm a very old friend of your mother's," said the fairy, "and now I'm going to be your friend. If you want to go to the King's ball, to the King's ball you shall go, or my name's not Benevola!"

"But I can't go in this dress," said Cinderella, looking down at her dreadful old clothes.

"Wash away your tears, my love," said the fairy, "and then we'll see."

So Cinderella had a good wash in the wooden bowl on the kitchen sink, and came back looking as fresh as a rose after rain.

"Now," said the fairy, "go at once to the end of the kitchen garden and bring me the biggest pumpkin you can find."

Cinderella took the stable lantern and went out. She came back with a great orange pumpkin, so big that she could hardly carry it.

"I'll run back for the lantern," she said.

"Do," said the fairy, "and at the same time get me the old rat who is asleep inside the bucket that stands by the well."

Cinderella went. She did not much like picking up the rat, but she did it, and he was quite kind and gentle, and did not try to bite or to run away.

"Now see if there are any mice in the trap in the old summer-house," said Benevola. There were six, and Cinderella brought them, running about briskly in the trap.

"Now six lizards from the lettuce bed," said the godmother; and these were caught and brought in in a handkerchief.

Then Benevola, standing there in her beautiful fairy clothes, waved her silver wand over Cinderella and her rags, and instantly her rags changed to a gown that was like white mist and diamond dew and silver moonshine, and on her head was a little crown of stars that shone among her dark hair.

Cinderella looked at herself in the polished lid of the brass preserving pan, and cried, "Can that be me? Oh, how pretty I am!" It was not one of the moments when grammar seems important.

"You are," said Benevola. "You're every inch a princess, my dear, like your dear mother before you. Let's see: have you got everything?—fan, gloves, handkerchief?"

Yes, Cinderella had them all.

"But my shoes," she said shyly, looking down at her poor old black slippers.

"Bless me! I nearly forgot the shoes," said the fairy. "Here they are—dear little magic glass ones. No one at the ball will dance like my goddaughter!" And she plunged her arm into her big pocket and pulled out a dear little pair of glass slippers. Real glass they were, and shone like the drops on a crystal chandelier. And yet they were soft as any kid glove.

"Put them on, my darling, and enjoy yourself in them," she said; "but remember you mustn't stay later than half-past eleven, or twenty to twelve at the very most, because the magic won't last after midnight. You'll remember, won't you?"

Cinderella promised to remember. Then Benevola set the pumpkin, the rat, the mice, and the lizards in the road opposite the front door, waved that wonderful wand of hers, and instantly the pumpkin was a golden coach more splendid than the King's, the mice were six white horses, the lizards six footmen in green and gold liveries, and the old rat was the stoutest and most respectable coachman who ever wore a three-cornered hat, and gold lace on his coat.

Cinderella kissed her godmother and thanked her again and again. Then she jumped into the coach and snuggled in among soft satin cushions. Benevola gave the order, "To the palace," and the white horses bounded forward.

In the palace everyone was enjoying himself very much indeed. All the ladies looked their very prettiest, and all the gentlemen thought so, and all the ladies knew that the gentlemen thought so. And when this is the case a party is usually a success.

One of the Court gentlemen, who had gone out to stand on the palace steps for a breath of fresh air, caught a glimpse of Cinderella, and rushed off to the Prince.

"I say, your Highness," he whispered, "the loveliest princess in all the world has just driven up in a golden coach drawn by six white horses. Oughtn't some one to go and welcome her?"

"*I* will," said Prince Charming eagerly; "there's no sense in disturbing the King and Queen."

And so it happened that Cinderella, in her dress of dew and mist and moonlight, was received at the very door of the palace by Prince Charming himself, in his Court suit of cloth of gold sewn with topazes. As he handed her up the marble steps of the grand staircase every one murmured, "What a handsome pair!"

But the Prince was saying to himself, "Oh, you dear little Princess! Oh, you pretty little Princess! I'll never marry any one but you—never, never, never!" While aloud, to her, he was saying the dullest, politest things about the weather, and the music, and the state of the roads that led to the palace.

Cinderella looked so lovely that no one could take their eyes off her, and even her unkind sisters, who did not recognise her in the least, owned that she was the most beautiful lady they had ever seen.

The Prince danced with her, and took her in to supper, and as the evening went on he began to talk of other things than the weather. He told her that her eyes were stars, and her mouth a flower, and things like that—quite silly things, because, of course, no one's eyes are like stars or their mouths like flowers—quite silly, but still she liked to hear them. And at last he said in that blunt, downright manner which is permitted to princes, "There is no one like you in the world. Will you marry me?"

She was just going to say, "Yes, please," for, indeed, she thought there was no one like *him* in the world, when the palace clock struck the half after eleven. She turned in a flash and ran down the corridor—and the magic glass slippers that had made her dancing the wonder of all the Court now made her running as swift as the wind's going, so that she had reached her coach and jumped in before the Prince, pursuing her, had turned the first corner in the grand staircase.

She got home just as the clock struck twelve, and at the last stroke coach and horses, coachman and footman, turned into what they had been before, and she herself was once more the shabby, dusty little Cinderella who had sat and cried into the ashes.

When her sisters came home she had to listen to their tales of the ball, and of the strange Princess who was so beautiful that she took everybody's breath away, and as she listened, yawning, she could hardly believe that she herself had really been that lovely lady.

She dreamed all night of the Prince. And next day the herald came round with the King's compliments, and would every one who had been at the ball last night kindly come round to the Palace again that evening?

And everything happened as before. The others drove off early, the fairy godmother came and waved her wand, and the Prince, anxiously watching at the head of the grand staircase, saw his Princess threading her way through the crowd like a moonbeam through dark water.

That night every one saw that it was going to be a match. The King and Queen were as pleased with Cinderella's pretty manners as Prince Charming was with her pretty face and the dear self that looked out of her eyes.

"Tell me your name, loveliest and dearest," he said. "Give me your hand and tell me the name of my bride."

And Cinderella, pale with happiness, and with eyes that really did look rather starry, gave him her hand and said:

"Dear Prince, my name is——" And then, boom, boom, boom!—the great clock in the palace tower began to strike midnight.

"Let me go—let me go!" cried Cinderella, and tore her hands from the Prince's, and ran, the magic slippers helping her all they could. But they could not help enough. Before she could get out of the palace grounds her beautiful dress had turned to rags, and as she reached the gate the only traces left of her grand coach and six and her fine servants were six scampering mice, six furtive lizards, a fat old running rat, and a big yellow pumpkin bowling along the road as hard as it could go, all by itself.

The night had changed its mind and turned out wet, and she had to run all the way home in the mud; and it was very difficult, because she had dropped one of her glass slippers in her haste to get away, and:

"You know how hard it is to run
With one shoe off and one shoe on."

When the Prince, wild with anxiety and disappointment, rushed out to ask the sentries about the magnificent Princess who had driven away, they told him that no one had passed out except a ragged beggar girl, running like a mad thing. So he went back to the palace with despair in his heart, and his dancing shoes wet through.

He did not sleep a wink all night, and next morning he sent for the herald, who was a very good fellow, and rather clever in his way.

"My dear herald," said the Prince, sitting on the edge of his bed in his blue satin dressing-gown sewn with seed-pearls, and waggling the toes of his gold-embroidered slippers, "you saw that strange Princess last night...? Well..."

"Bless you, your Highness," said the herald, who was about the same age as the Prince, "I know all about it. Lost lady. Love of a life. No expense spared. Return and all will be forgotten and forgiven. You want to find her?"

"I should think I did!"

"Well, it's quite simple. What's that sparklety thing sticking out of the breast pocket of your dressing-gown?"

"Yes," said the Prince oddly, and drew out Cinderella's slipper.

"Well, then!" said the herald, and unfolded his idea, which pleased Prince Charming so much that within an hour the herald had set out, with the glass slipper borne before him on a blue cushion with a fringe of peacock's feathers, and the trumpets blowing like grampuses, and the pennons flying like pretty pigeons all about him, to find the lady whose foot that slipper would fit. For in those days shoes were not sold ready-made in shops, but were made specially to fit the people who were to wear them. And besides, the glass slipper was magic, and so had too much sense to have fitted any one but its owner, even if the country had been full of shops selling Rats' Ready-made Really Reliable Boots.

The herald called at every house, great and small, and every girl in every house had to try on the slipper. At last, when it was evening, and he was getting very tired of the whole business, and was beginning to wish that shoes had never been invented at all, he came to the house where Cinderella lived.

Blow, blow! went the trumpets; flutter, flutter, went the pennons; and the herald's voice, rather faint and husky, cried:

"Oyez, oyez, oyez! Prince Charming offers his hand and heart to the lady who can wear this little glass slipper. Who'll try? Who'll try? Who'll try? Will ye try? Will ye try? Will ye try, try, try?" So that he sounded like a butcher in the Old Kent Road of a Saturday night, only they say "buy" instead of "try."

Dressalinda and Marigolda pushed and hustled Cinderella to make her open the door quickly. She was quite as anxious as they were to open it, for reasons of her own—reasons which you know as well as she did.

So the door was thrown open, and in came the herald, and the trumpeters and men-at-arms grouped themselves picturesquely about the doorsteps, to the envy and admiration of the neighbours.

Dressalinda sat down in the big carved chair in the hall, and stuck out a large stout foot.

"No good," said the herald. "I'm sorry, miss. It's a fine foot—as fine as ever I saw—but it's not just the cut for the glass slipper."

And even Dressalinda had to own that it wasn't.

Then Marigolda tried. And though she had had time to slip upstairs and put on her best fine silk stockings the little glass slipper would not begin to go on to her long flat foot.

"It's the heel, miss," said the herald. "I'm sorry, but it's not my fault, nor yours either. We can't help our heels, nor yet other people's. So now for the other girl."

"What other girl?" "There *is* no other girl," said the two sisters together.

But the herald said, "What about the one who opened the door?"

"Oh, that was only Cinderella," "Just a kitchen wench," said Marigolda and Dressalinda, tossing their heads.

"There's many a pretty foot under a ragged skirt," said the herald; and he went to the top of the kitchen stairs, and called "Cinderella! Cinderella!"—not because he thought it at all possible that the slipper would fit a kitchen wench, but because he had undertaken to try it on *all* girls. Also, he disliked the elder sisters as much as any one possibly could on so short an acquaintance. When you knew them better, of course, it was different.

So poor Cinderella came, all ragged and dusty, but with her bright beauty shining through the dust and the rags like the moon through clouds. And the herald knew that she was the lost Princess, even before she slipped on the little glass shoe, pulled the other one from her pocket, slipped that on too, and stood up in the pair of them.

"Found!" cried the herald. "Oh, joy! the long-lost Princess! You are to come with me at once to the palace."

"I can't come like this," said Cinderella, looking at her rags. "I can't, and I won't!"

But the fairy godmother appeared most opportunely from the cupboard under the stairs where the boots and galoshes were kept, and with one wave of her wand clothed Cinderella from head to foot in cloth-of-splendour.

Then Cinderella looked at her unkind sisters, and said timidly, "Goodbye."

And the sisters looked at her, and frowned, and "Goodbye" said they.

Then the fairy smiled, and, pointing her wand at them, said, "Speak the truth." And there in the presence of Cinderella and the fairy and the herald and each other and the hat-and-umbrella-stand they had to speak it.

"I have been very unkind and hateful to Cinderella," said Dressalinda, "and I am very sorry. I have been sorry since the night before last, but I was ashamed to say so. I am sorry because on that night I lost my heart to a good gentleman, who lost his to me, and I hate the thought of all the wickedness that makes me unworthy of him."

"That's right," said the herald kindly. "'A fault that's owned, is half atoned.' And what does the other lady say?"

"I say the same as my sister," said Marigolda, "and I hope Cinderella will forgive us."

"Of course I do," said Cinderella heartily. So that was settled.

They all went to Court—the fairy godmother made the pumpkin coach again in a moment—and Prince Charming met Cinderella at the steps of the palace, and kissed her before the whole crowd there assembled, and every one cheered, and a chorus of invisible fairies sang:

> *"Take her, O Prince, faithful and true;*
> *That little foot was just made for the shoe.*
> *We are so glad! Every one knew*
> *That little Princess was just made for you.*
>
> *"Shout for the pair, Army and Fleet!*
> *Lonely policeman, hurrah on your beat!*
> *May life be long, joy be complete,*
> *Rose-strewn the path of those dear little feet!"*

The two noble gentlemen rushed forward, as soon as politeness to the Prince allowed, to greet their dear ladies, who had been the wicked sisters, and who now were so sorry and ashamed, because love had taught them to wish to be good.

They were all married the next day, and when Marigolda and Dressalinda confessed to their father how horrid they had been to Cinderella, he said, "Dear, dear! And I never noticed! How remiss of me!" and went back to his books.

But the cruel step-mother, who had brought up her children so badly, and who was not sorry at all, was sent to a Home for the Incurably Unkind. She is treated kindly, but she is not allowed the chance of being unkind to any one else.

And Cinderella and Charming and the sisters and their husbands all lived exactly as long as was good for them, and loved each other more and more every day of their lives. And no one can ask for a better fate than that!

BEAUTY AND THE BEAST

THERE WAS ONCE a rich merchant, who had a "town house replete with every modern convenience," and a "country house standing in its own grounds of seventeen acres, agreeably situated in the most delightful rural scenery, with vineries, pineries, conservatories, palm-houses, stabling, piggeries, henneries, and accommodation for 300,000 full-grown bees." At least, that is what the auctioneer said about the houses when he came to sell them. For the merchant was unlucky. A great storm swept the sea and wrecked his six ships, that were coming home to him full of priceless stuffs; a band of robbers attacked his caravans as they came across the desert laden with the richest gems of the East. It was all quite sudden. He went to bed rich, happy, and contented. He opened his newspaper next morning, and in half a minute knew that he was a ruined man. His debts, though not more than a man in his position is accustomed to incur, and is able to pay in due course, were enough to swallow up all the money he had in the bank, as well as what he got by the sale of the two houses and all the rest of it, including his horses and carriages, and the beautiful clothes and jewels of his three daughters. Their mother had died years before, and now for the first time their father was glad of it. "At least," he said, *"she* will not have to suffer the pinch of poverty."

His daughters, however, had to suffer it with him. The two elder ones, as is usual in fairy stories, were proud, vain, and unattractive. They had had several offers of marriage, because it was known that their father would give them a good dowry, but they had refused every offer with scorn. Nothing short of an admiral or a duke would satisfy their ambition, and dukes were scarce just then, and all the admirals were already married. The youngest daughter was so lovely that from her childhood she had been called "Beauty." She was as pretty as a picture, and as good as she was pretty. Every one, except her sisters, agreed that she was a perfect dear.

A few of the merchant's old friends clubbed together and bought him a cottage in the country, and made him a present of enough money every year for him and his daughters to live on, if he was very careful. It was a nice little house, called Rose Cottage, with a vine and climbing honeysuckle and jasmine growing all over it, and there was a good garden, with fruit trees and flowers.

"Now," said the merchant cheerfully, when they were dumped down with a few odds and ends of furniture in the empty cottage, "the world is full of ups and downs, and we are in the downs just now. If we are to live here comfortably we must all work, for we can't afford a servant."

"*We* won't work," said the two elder sisters. "It's too much to expect us to soil our hands with anything so low as *work*."

"My dears," said the merchant, "if we do have to work for a year or two, it's only what nine-tenths of our fellow creatures have to do all their lives long. And Fortune's wheel will very likely take another turn, if we're patient, and lift us up again."

But the elder sisters only sniffed superior, and sat apart in a window-seat, remarking on the smallness of the honeysuckle and the poor quality of the jasmine flowers, while Beauty and her father arranged the furniture, got the beds ready, swept up the dust and straw scattered by the men who had done the removing, set the table, and cooked some steak for supper.

The sisters did nothing but grumble, even saying that the steak was tough, which it wasn't, and that the plates were not clean, which they were.

And as they began so they went on. They spent all their time in reading and re-reading a lot of odd numbers of the *Real Lady's Home Journal,* which an old housemaid had sent them out of pity, and trying to imagine new dresses, silks and satins and lace—to be made from the cut-out paper patterns given away with the *Real Lady.*

The merchant took off his coat and turned up his shirt sleeves and went to work like a man. He cleaned the boots and knives, carried coals, blacked the grates, drew water from the well, and did all the heavy work that women ought never to be allowed to do. Besides all that, he kept the garden in perfect order, so that not a weed showed its head there, and lupins, leopard's bane, larkspur, gardener's garters, goat's rue, columbines, poppies and lilies and sweet williams all grew as if they had been born there. But there were no roses, and, of course, there was no money to spare for rose-bushes. I suppose it was called Rose Cottage so as to have at least one "rose" there—on the gate-post, where the name was painted.

Beauty, for her part, kept the house clean and pretty, washed, starched, ironed, baked, brewed, and sewed, and she and her father were as happy as the days were long, except for the grumblings of the sisters, and even these the two workers got used to in time, so that they hardly noticed them—just as people who live near a railway get used to the rattling and screaming and thundering of the trains, and people who live in towns get used to the voices of poor people saying, "I am starving. Give me a penny, for the love of God!" You'll agree with me that if you can get used to the noise of railways and the voices of your starving brothers you can get used to anything. So the disagreeableness of the sisters almost ceased to be a worry, and everything went on getting pleasanter and pleasanter for a year—and it came to be jasmine-time again.

And then one morning when Beauty was shaking the door-mats at the front gate, with a blue handkerchief over her head to keep the dust from her hair, the postman came along the road; and oh, wonderful! he had a letter in his hand—the first they had had since they came to live at Rose Cottage.

"It's for your father," said the postman. "Thank God for a beautiful day."

"Yes," said Beauty, and took the letter to her father, who was digging a dish of new potatoes for dinner.

He opened it.

"What is it?" asked Beauty, for he looked glad.

He did not answer. And "*Oh*, what is it?" Beauty asked, for now he looked sorry.

"I almost wish it hadn't happened," he said slowly, scraping the earth off the fork with the edge of his boot. "For we've been very happy together here, my Beauty. But I suppose I ought to go—if it's only for the sake of your poor sisters." He handed her the letter, which told how two of the merchant's ships, which were supposed to be lost, had come safely to port, laden with rich treasure, so that he was now a wealthy man again; and please would he hurry up and take his goods away, for they were littering up the quays, and the Municipal Council could not allow the roadway to be obstructed by the strewn-about bales of any merchant.

Well, of course he set out at once. The two sisters got up, half dressed and with their hair in curl-papers, to say goodbye to him. Beauty gave him a good breakfast; and if she did drop a tear or two into his coffee cup as she filled it, nobody was the worse or the wiser.

"Goodbye, my dears," he said, as he stood by the gate waiting for the coach. "I'll bring you each a present. What would you like?"

"A purse full of money—quite full," said the eldest.

"A casket of jewels," said the second.

"And what shall I bring for my Beauty?" the old man asked fondly, for she had said nothing.

"Oh, bring me a rose," said Beauty, who didn't want him to bother about presents for her, when she knew how busy he would be clearing up his bales and things.

But when he came to the city he found that there were no ships, and no bales, and no anything at all for him but disappointment. The letter was just a hoax, planned by some of the young men whom the elder sisters had treated so rudely long ago. He shrugged his shoulders and turned to go home again, not too unhappy, after all, because he had still his best treasure at home—his dear Beauty.

He found that no coach went past Rose Cottage till next morning, and he was afraid that if he did not get home that night Beauty would be unhappy and anxious, so he decided to travel by the Flying Serpent, a coach which would set him down about tea-time at a town ten miles from home. He would walk those ten miles and be home for supper.

And sure enough he started to walk those ten miles. But he did not get home to supper.

Thinking of Beauty and of his pleasant, busy life with her, he forgot to read the sign-posts with proper care, and so wandered quite out of the right road. The path got rough and stony, and the boughs of the trees hung low over it. At last even the absent-minded merchant could not help seeing that it was not the high-road that he was on. Also he now noticed that it was nearly dark—so dark that he could not see to read the next sign-post, and had actually to climb up it before he could make out that it was trying to say to him, "This is the right way."

He was quite sure that the sign-post was wrong, but there did not seem to be any other that knew better, so he went on, quite soon through inky darkness, only guided by a blue light that shone ahead like a sick star. It led him through a garden, where he stumbled among trellises and against statues, and blundered up steps, till at last he came to a great house; and over its front door was the blue lamp that had guided him.

He knocked, but as no one answered he lifted the latch and went in. There was a hall, beautiful and big, and beyond that another, still bigger and more beautiful. This hall had a pleasant wood fire, and a sideboard loaded with the nicest kind of cold supper. A little table near the fire was laid for one.

The merchant ventured to sit down by the fire and try to dry himself. He looked longingly at the pleasant things on the sideboard, and at last he could not bear his hunger any longer, for he had had nothing since breakfast. "When the master of the house comes in I'm sure he will forgive me," he said, and instantly ate a cold partridge. Then he had some pickled salmon, a game pie, three fat buns, some cherry pie, and a cream cheese. Then he did not feel so hungry, but he was strangely sleepy, so he looked about for a place to rest, and, finding a nice little room opening out of the hall, he pulled off his wet clothes and crept between the cool clean sheets and fell fast asleep.

The sun woke him next morning. A bath was set out ready for him, and also a new suit of clothes exactly like his old ones.

"Oh, I see," he said, "this is a poor-house, where the State takes care of poor travellers who haven't money to spend on hotels. I am very lucky to have found it. And how delicately it's all done! The Guardians of the Poor arrange everything so beautifully, and then keep out of the way to avoid being thanked." When he had had breakfast in the hall, still seeing no one, he started to walk home, and on his way through the gardens he remembered Beauty's wish, and stopped to gather her a rose from one of the flower-covered trellises.

Then suddenly with a fierce and frightening howl a great shaggy beast leapt out from behind a magnolia tree, and shook a knobbly club in his face.

"Ungrateful wretch!" growled the Beast. "You have been treated like a prince in my house, and in return you steal my roses. Prepare to die."

"Oh, please don't!" said the merchant. "I am so sorry. I never meant… Oh, my lord, spare me!"

"I'm not a lord—I'm a beast," said the creature; and so he was—something between a bear and a hyena, with a dash of monkey and something of the elephant.

"Good Beast," said the merchant through chattering teeth, "I only just took one rose for my daughter. She is so fond of roses."

"How many daughters have you?" asked the Beast.

"Three," said the merchant. "Oh, spare me for their sakes!"

"Very well," said the Beast, "I'll let you off this time if one of your daughters will come here and die instead of you. That's all I have to say. Good-morning. If you or your daughter aren't here by tea-time tomorrow—I shall call at your house and take the whole family."

"I am at your mercy," said the poor merchant. "I will come back myself tomorrow, in plenty of time for your tea. Of course, I sha'n't allow my daughters to sacrifice themselves for me."

"Humph!" said the Beast. "I'll order a carriage for you— you'll get home quicker; and it can call for you tomorrow and bring you back—you or your daughter."

The carriage was very comfortable, but the merchant was on thorns. The only comfort was that the Beast had insisted on his taking a big chest of gold, and the thought that this was now on the box beside the coachman, and would presently be a handsome dowry and livelihood for his daughters, consoled him a little.

When he got home he sent away the carriage, and kissed his children.

"What's in the chest, father?" said the elder ones, speaking both at once and in a very great hurry. "Is it our presents?"

"It is the money for you to live on when I am dead," said the father. "That is the only present I have brought; that and this rose for my Beauty, which has cost her father's life."

And he told them what had happened.

"Ah," said the eldest sister, "this is your doing! If you hadn't tried to be so extra humble and unselfish *this* wouldn't have happened. You might at least cry, like us."

"I've nothing to cry about," said Beauty, hugging her father; "it's my rose, and I'm going to pay for it."

"I shouldn't dream of allowing such a thing," said the merchant crossly.

"I'd much sooner die all in a minute," said Beauty, "than be miserable all my life long at the thought that I'd caused my father's death."

"Nonsense," said her father. "I shall go back tomorrow, as I said."

"If you do," said Beauty, "I shall go with you. And if you go without me, I shall follow you."

"You're a naughty, obstinate girl," said the merchant angrily; and then he burst into tears, and caught her in his arms, and said she was his dear love and his own treasure. You see, he was rather upset.

Beauty got her father to herself while the sisters examined the chest.

"I will hang myself down the well the minute you're gone if you leave me behind," said she; and that settled it.

"After all," said the merchant, "he may spare you more readily than me. How could any one be beast enough to hurt even a hair of your dear head?"

And so it happened that just about tea-time Beauty and her father arrived at the Beast's mansion. There was no one about, but food was put ready as before. When the merchant saw this he began to be more cheerful, and, having been there already, felt almost at home, and showed Beauty the fine furniture and rich hangings as though he had invented them himself. "See," he said, "how beautifully everything is arranged for us. Here's your room, next to mine—see, 'Beauty's Bedroom' set on the door in pearls. He'd never have gone to all this trouble and expense if he meant to kill you. Now come to supper, my child. The game pies here are first-rate!"

So they had supper together, and each, by trying to cheer up the other, cheered himself up at the same time, as so often happens.

They slept well, and next morning it was actually pleasant to walk in the rose-garden. They could not believe that the owner of this beautiful house, who had shown them such hospitality, could really mean to kill either of them. And they were right, as people so often are when they look upon the bright side of things.

For the Beast appeared from behind the magnolia so suddenly that Beauty could not help giving one little scream.

"Don't be afraid," said the Beast, in tones so gentle as to sound extremely odd from that great shaggy, fierce-toothed mouth. "Don't be afraid. No one is going to hurt you. Do you come of your own free will?"

"Yes—oh, yes," said Beauty.

"Thank you," said the Beast; "you're a good girl. Now, Sir Merchant, goodbye; and if you come back I shall certainly make you sorry for it."

The merchant had to go. And when the carriage which took him away was out of sight the Beast turned to Beauty and said:

"All my house is yours, but the west wing is especially your own. See, there is a door that leads straight into it from the rose-garden. I shall not bore you with my company, for I know quite well how stupid I am; but I hope you'll allow me to see you once a day, for a few moments after supper."

He bowed, as politely as any beast could, and left her; and Beauty, of course, instantly explored the west wing. All the rooms were furnished exactly as she would have furnished her home herself if she had had the money. There were good books, good pictures, beautiful carvings, soft carpets and curtains of her favourite colours, lutes and pear-drums and guitars, flowers in every room, and in every room the air of welcome which is the most charming of all furniture.

And in her boudoir was a mirror as big as the side of a state-coach, and in it she could see anything she chose to wish to see. She wished to see her father, and saw him leaning back in the carriage, with tears running down his face.

This made her cry too, and she had no heart to explore her house further; but presently she said, "Come, Beauty, don't be a silly little coward," and dried her eyes and went and practised for an hour at the harpsichord.

After supper that night the violet velvet curtain that hung over the door stirred and was lifted. There stood the Beast.

"May I come in?" he said.

"Yes," said Beauty, resolved not to be frightened.

"I am very ugly, am I not?" said the Beast.

"You are, rather," said Beauty, "but you are very kind to me."

"I am ugly, and I am stupid," said he. "In fact, I am a perfect beast."

"Nobody's really stupid if they know they're not clever," said Beauty.

"I hope you'll be happy here," said he.

"You are very kind," said she.

"I can't think of anything else to say," said the Beast, "except one thing."

"What's that?" said Beauty, encouragingly.

"Beauty, will you marry me?" said he.

"No, thank you, Beast," said Beauty.

And he sighed and walked heavily out of the room on his great hairy beast-feet.

Every night he came to see her, and every night tried to talk, but the only really interesting thing he ever said was, "Beauty, will you marry me?" He said that every night; and every night Beauty said, "No, thank you, Beast."

This went on for three months, and then one morning when Beauty looked in the mirror, as she always did, to see how her father was getting on, she saw him ill in bed, and her sisters just starting off, very gaily dressed, for a water-picnic; for the Beast's money had provided them with the kind of friends that money can buy.

She looked for the Beast everywhere that day, but could not find him. At supper-time he came as usual, and was horrified to find her with red eyes, and swollen nose, and all the marks of having cried most of the day.

"What is it, my dear Beauty, my Dear?" he cried. "Do you really hate me so? Are you so unhappy with me? Very well; go. I can bear anything rather than to see you cry. Leave me. I cannot live without you—but I would rather die than keep you against your will."

"Indeed, indeed," said Beauty, "I wasn't crying for that. I *am* fond of you, really I am, though I can't marry you. And I should be quite contented to stay here for ever with you. But my father is ill."

Then she told him what she had seen in the mirror.

"Let me go home for a week," she said, "and I'll faithfully come back at the end."

"I will—oh, I will," said the Beast. "How can I refuse you anything that you ask me, however much I suffer? Take this ruby ring, put it on your right hand when you go to bed tonight, and you'll wake up in your old home. On the last night of the week put it on your left hand, and you'll wake up here. And remember, dear Beauty, if you don't come back it will kill me."

Beauty did as she was told, and next morning awoke in her own little white bedroom, with the red vine tendrils looking in at the window.

She found her father ill, but she kissed him better in five minutes, for he was only ill of grief at the loss of her. And by the end of the week he was as well as ever.

Now though the magic ring that brought Beauty home had also brought two chests of fine clothes and jewels, and though Beauty had given nearly all these things to her sisters, yet still they hated her and cursed her. So they made a wicked plot, and put sleepy herbs in her supper chocolate, so that she slept without waking for thirty-six hours.

"Now she has broken her word," said the elder, "and the Beast will kill her when she does go back."

Beauty did not know that she had missed a day, and put on the ring a day late, without knowing it. She woke in her pearl and white room at the Beast's house—and only then did she know that she had broken her word, and had stayed away for more than the week. She knew it by the date marked by the calendar of living roses, that changed, all of its own live cleverness, every day. She remembered then the queer taste of the supper chocolate, and how drowsy and ill she had felt in the morning, and she guessed the truth.

"He will have thought me faithless," she said; "he will have been very unhappy. But he'll forgive me at supper-time, when I tell him all about it."

And the day seemed as though it would never be done. She longed for supper-time, to tell all about it and be forgiven.

Supper-time came at last, but no Beast. Beauty grew more and more anxious and unhappy. She had put on the loveliest of all the lovely dresses that the Beast had given her, so as to please the eyes that she knew loved to see her beauty beautifully set. She waited and waited and waited till the clock struck eleven, and then she could bear it no longer. She caught up her white satin train and ran through all the rooms of the mansion, calling:

"Beast! Beast! Where are you?"

And nothing answered her but the desolate echoes of the empty house.

Then she ran out into the garden, and up and down the rose walks and the jasmine alleys, where still the flowers were blooming in summer glory, though everywhere else it was chill October. And now she cried, "Beast, dear Beast, where are you?"

And still there came no answer.

The splendour of the full moon lighted the gardens as with a pale dream-daylight. As she ran down the grass alley where the statues stood she saw by the fountain something dark that lay along the ground against the white marble of the fountain's basin.

In a moment she was leaning over it. It was the Beast. Dead! Dead? No—but hardly living; yet she could feel his heart beat faintly through his thick fur.

She sank down on the dewy grass, pulled his head on to her lap, and put her arms round his shaggy neck.

"Oh, Beast, dearest, don't die," she sobbed. "I can't bear it if you die. I can't live without you. It wasn't my fault I was late—oh, believe me it wasn't! Oh, don't die, dearest—don't die and leave me!"

The Beast opened his sad eyes and looked at her.

"I'm dying, Beauty," he said, so low that she could hardly hear him. "You don't love me. This is only pity. Goodbye."

"Not love you!" cried Beauty. "Oh, dearest, can't you see that I'm crying my eyes out? Only live, and you shall see whether I love you!"

Then the Beast once again put the old question, very faint, very hopeless.

"Beauty," he said, "will you marry me?"

"Ah!" said Beauty, "that I will!" And she tightened her arms round his neck and kissed him between the eyes.

Then in a moment the whole house glowed with light—coloured lamps hung like magic fruit from all the trees; and in her arms instead of the Beast's head was the head of the handsomest prince in the world. He sprang to his feet and kneeled before her.

"You have given me life, and love," he said. "I was changed to a beast by wicked fairies, and condemned to be a beast till someone should truly love me. Dearest, we shall be the happiest couple in the world!"

They were. The old father made his home with them; but the wicked sisters, as soon as they breathed the air of that garden, were turned to stone. Their hearts were stone already, and the rest was easy to the good fairy who had watched over the Beast and led his dear Beauty to him.

They stand as statues at the lodge gates of that mansion to this day.

JACK THE GIANT-KILLER

IN THE LONG-AGO days of King Arthur, who invented round tables, there was a sort of plague of giants in the West Country—just as nowadays there are plagues of wasps, and mosquitoes, and millionaires; and the giants threatened to spread, like other plagues, till they had eaten up all nice, proper-sized people in England. But this dreadful thing did not happen, because there was a boy named Jack, who cared for nothing in the world but killing giants. Now when a boy—or a girl either, for that matter— cares only for one thing, that is the thing it will do, and do well. Jack did so well at the giant-killing that though he lived hundreds and hundreds of years ago, yet to this day whenever people speak of "The Giant-Killer" every one knows that they mean Jack, and could not possibly mean anyone else.

From the time when Jack was quite little he used to listen (with his mouth open) to the stories that grown-up people told as they sat round the wood fire on winter nights, or lounged of a summer evening on the village green. In those days people had no books to read, and couldn't have read them if they had had them, so that stories were remembered, and told again and again. And among the stories that Jack heard, of dragons and enchanters and witches and fairies, were stories of giants, and these were the tales he loved. When the other children, playing on the smooth sea-sand between the rocks, took sticks and tried to draw men and women and dogs and horses, it was always giants that Jack wanted to draw, and this needed so much room that the other children used to tell him to go away and find a bit of sand of his own to draw on. They liked it better when Jack divided the boys of the village into two bands, and they all played at battles and sieges among the rocks and caves, exactly as boys do now.

His father, who kept the ferry-boat at the mouth of the river, sometimes used to say, "When Jack grows up he shall be a ferry-man"; and then Jack never said a word, good or bad, but in his heart he used to say, "When I grow up I will be a giant-killer."

It happened, however, that he was to be what he wished to be, even before he grew up.

One night as he and his father were sitting by the fire waiting for supper to be ready—a very nice supper of boiled shoulder of kid, with leeks and onions—an enormous hand came down the chimney, lifted the lid off the pot, and flung it rattling and hissing among the wood ashes. Then a great finger and thumb picked the meat out of the broth, and meat and hand disappeared up the chimney.

"Hullo!" said Jack, "there's nice manners for you!"

"You don't expect manners from giants," said Jack's father. "I know who it is that's stolen our supper. I heard there was a giant called Cormoran, come to live on the mountain, but I never thought he'd demean himself to take our poor little bit of supper. Why, they say he makes nothing of going home with a dozen oxen over his shoulder, and a few score of swine strung on a bough, as we string herrings on a withy."

"Does he so?" said Jack. "Well, he has taken our supper, and left us only a leeky swill of broth to comfort our stomachs withal. There shall be a reckoning to pay for this same supper."

"Big words, my boy," said his father, "big words! Sop your bread and sup your broth, and get you to bed, for bread and broth's all our supper this night."

Jack sopped his bread and supped his broth, and got to bed; but he did not get to sleep. He knew there was some way of doing what he meant to do, and there should be no sleep for him till he found that way. And before dawn the way was found. Jack got up from his tossed bed of dry forest leaves, took his father's lanthorn, and a pickaxe, and a horn. Then out he went to the mountain his father had told him of; and there was the castle where the giant lived whose great red hand had come down the chimney and taken the meat out of the pot.

Jack stopped about a hundred yards from the castle gates and began to dig; and I think that pickaxe must have been a magic one, because before dawn he had dug a pit twenty feet deep and ten feet wide. Then he cut trees down—no doubt with the magic pickaxe—and covered up the pit with the branches, and strewed earth and loose grass and stones, and made everything look as though it were solid ground.

Then he ran back a dozen paces and blew on his horn, looking up at the castle windows in the chill grey of the dawn.

The giant inside the castle was not used to getting up so early in the morning, for he was a luxurious dog, and often lay in bed as late as nine o'clock. He put his big ugly head out of the castle window—the one that was over the front door—and saw Jack dancing about a little way down the mountain blowing like mad on his aggravating horn.

"You saucy scoundrel!" said the giant. "You shall pay for this. I'll grill you for my breakfast."

And next minute the heavy door opened, and out came the giant. Jack just laughed, and the giant strode down the mountain shaking a fist at him as big as a leg of Leicester mutton.

And next minute, crash! smash! the boughs broke under his weight, and there was the giant in the pit Jack had dug for him.

"What now?" cried Jack, still laughing. "Will nothing serve you for breakfast but poor little Jack?"

And with that he hit the top of the enormous head with the pickaxe, and so Giant Cormoran came by his death.

Then Jack ran to the town just as people were beginning to open their shops and sweep in front of their doors, and he climbed to the top of the market cross, and from there told the good news to the people who crowded round.

All the justices and persons of importance, when they came to know what Jack had done, decided that he ought to have a reward, so they gave him a sword of blue steel, and a squire's belt, and on the belt the young ladies of the town worked in gold thread certain words:

> *"This is the valiant Cornishman*
> *Who killed the giant Cormoran."*

So Jack went home to his father very proud and happy, but less inclined than ever to be a ferry-man.

Now everyone was talking of Jack's courage and cleverness, and a giant named Blunderbore took an oath before seven other giants who happened to be dining with him at Easter that he would kill Jack and avenge Cormoran's death.

And Jack heard of it, and kept out of the way. But when October came, and Blunderbore was brewing his autumn ale, he went to the river with a tub to get water for his brewing, and by the river lay Jack, fast asleep.

The giant knew him by the words on his belt, so he picked him up very gently with his finger and thumb, and carried him off to the enchanted castle in a wood, which was Blunderbore's home, and Jack woke up to find himself where he had no wish to be. For the giant flung him into a horrible room half filled with the bones of his victims, and said:

"You are going to be my supper, and I am going to fetch a friend to sup with me."

He started off, and Jack, left alone, set his wits to work. From every side came shrieks of poor people shut up in other dungeons, and this worried him a good deal. But it did not prevent his seeing that two stout cords hung from pulleys to a beam in the roof.

Jack made a running noose in each cord, and watched through the window, and when the two giants came along arm in arm he dropped the two ropes over their two giant heads just as they were coming in at the door. Then he pulled away till both were strangled, and that was the end of *them*. He slid down one of the ropes and stabbed each of the giants with his sword, to make sure, and then he took the keys out of Blunderbore's pocket and set all the other poor prisoners free.

Then he started to go home again, but the giant had carried him a long way, and now it was quite dark, and he was still far from the ferry. So, coming to a comfortable-looking house, he knocked at the door to ask for a night's lodging. And who should open the door but a giant—that was the sort of thing that *would* happen to Jack—and the giant had two heads.

However, both heads nodded, and the two mouths smiled in a friendly way, and he took Jack in, gave him pork and beans for supper, and showed him a bedroom with a good bed in it, and plenty of blankets for coverings.

But Jack had no sleep in his eyes, and as he lay awake he heard the giant in the next room mumbling to himself, and presently he heard what it was that the giant was saying. It was this:

> *"Although ye lodge with me this night,*
> *Ye shall not see the morning's light—*
> *My club shall smash your brains outright."*

This was not a soothing lullaby, and Jack felt less sleepy than ever.

"Fair and soft," said he; "so these are your pleasant ways with poor travellers! I must try a match with you, my kind host."

He got up, and felt about in the dark for a big log of rotten wood that he had noticed on the hearth, put it on the bed, and covered it up in the blankets. Then he hid himself in the corner of the room behind some old saddles and sacks of hard pears.

It was just as well he did, for before long the giant came in and beat on the bed with his great club till he thought he had killed his visitor.

Therefore the giant was very much surprised when, the next morning, Jack tapped at his door and thanked him for his night's lodging.

"Bless my body!" said the giant (whose name was Red Morgan), "is it you? And how did you sleep last night? Did anything disturb you?"

"Oh, no," said Jack. "I slept sound enough; only once a rat or suchlike ran over the bed and tickled my nose with its tail."

The giant scratched his two red heads, for he was very much perplexed.

"Well," he said, "come you down to breakfast."

The breakfast was hasty pudding, and while the giant was ladling it out of the big black pot on the hearth Jack tied his leathern wallet round his neck so that it hung out of sight, between his shirt and his skin.

Then, as fast as he could, he spooned up the hot pudding, pretending to put it in his mouth, but really he dropped it nearly all into the wallet.

"Dear heart alive!" said Red Morgan, who was Welsh, "you eat as much as hur can hurself."

"That's nothing," said Jack. "I can do more than you can, good sir. I can walk on my little fingers with my heels in the air. I can cut off my head and stick it on again. I can rip up my paunch and bring back all your hasty pudding!"

And with that he slit open the wallet with his knife, and two or three quarts of hasty pudding blobbed out upon the floor.

"Odds splutterkins!" said the giant, "hur can do that hurself!"

So saying, he plunged his great knife into his own fat stomach, and fell down on the stone floor as dead as mutton. Thus Jack settled yet another giant.

Jack's next adventure he had in the company of King Arthur's only son, whom he chanced to meet when the Prince was on his way to rescue a lovely lady from the power of a magician. They agreed to travel together, and as the Prince was very kind and gave to all the poor who asked, the two presently found themselves without money for a night's lodging.

Jack, never at a loss, stopped at the first giant's house they came to—the country seems to have been full of such houses—hid the Prince in a hollow tree, and knocked at the big front door. The giant put his head out of the window and said, "Who's there?" just as you or I might if someone came to the door very late.

"It's only your poor little cousin Jack," said the giant-killer.

"Well, what's the best news, cousin," said the giant.

"There's nothing but bad news," said Jack. "King Arthur has conquered all his enemies, and just to keep his hands warm he is sending his son to kill you and throw down your strong towers."

"Fiddlededee!" said the giant. "He can't do it."

"Oh, cousin," said Jack, "but he has two thousand soldiers with swords and two thousand men with battering-rams."

"That's a very different pair of shoes, Cousin Jack," said the giant. "Come in and hide me in the stone cellar till they are gone. Blood's thicker than water, and cousins should help each other."

So Jack locked the giant in the stone cellar, and then, of course, he and the Prince had the run of the house and larder. They ate well, and drank well, and slept in the giant's best bed with the tapestry hangings.

Next morning the two threw bread and bones about, and slopped red wine on the table and among the rushes on the floor, to make believe that many had been feasting. Then the Prince set out alone, and Jack lighted a torch at the kitchen embers, and went to let out the giant.

He seems to have been a nice gentle, grateful giant, and I suppose Jack thought so too, for he did not try any of his deceitful giant-killing tricks here. Only when the giant had thanked him again and again for his kind help, and said, "How can I reward you?" Jack replied:

"Give me only the old coat and cap and the old shoes, and the rusty sword and belt that hang under the tester of your best bed."

Then the giant laughed, and said, "You are as crafty as I am big. Well, well, take them. The coat's the coat of darkness, and when you wear it no one can see you; the cap is the cap of knowledge, and will show you all things; the shoes are the shoes of swiftness—no one can catch you when you run in them; and the sword is the sword of sharpness, and will cut through iron bars as easy as through a nettle-stalk. Take them, Cousin Jack, and my blessing with them; and so goodbye, cousin."

These four gifts made it an easy matter to find the magician, cut off his head, and free the Prince's lady; and when this was done the three went to Court, and the Prince and the lady were married, and Jack was made a Knight of the Round Table.

But Jack wanted more adventures; so he set out, and had the good luck to meet a giant who was carrying away a knight and a lady. This giant also he killed, and then sought out the giant's twin brother, who lived in a cave, and finished him off too, all in one day. It was mere child's-play now to Jack, killing giants, because he had the wonderful coat and sword and shoes and cap.

Then he went and supped with the knight and the lady in their castle. There was a splendid banquet, and the harper made a great song of Jack's mighty deeds, and the knight gave him a gold ring with a picture on the bezel of the giant carrying off the knight and the lady.

And just when everything was at its jolliest a white-faced messenger rushed in and cried out in a terrible voice that the great two-headed Cornish giant, Thundel, was coming to avenge the death of his cousins, whom Jack had killed that day. Instantly all was confusion. The archers ran to the narrow windows; the crossbow men took up their station on the battlements. Some ran to raise the drawbridge, others to lower the portcullis, and yet others made haste to heat lead to pour through the holes in the great gateway.

But Jack said, "Now you shall see some sport."

He ordered the men to let down the drawbridge and saw it nearly in two in the middle. Then he put on the coat of darkness and the shoes of swiftness, and went out to meet the giant, who came lumbering along, shaking the earth as he came, and sniffling and turning his two heads this way and that. He cried out in a voice as big as a church-bell's voice:

> "Fee, foh, fah, fum,
> I smell the blood of an Englishman;
> Be he alive or be he dead,
> I'll grind his bones to make my bread."

"You must catch your bird before you cook him," said Jack, and pulled off his coat and ran. The giant ran clumsily after him, and Jack ran three times round the moat, just to show off, and then over the drawbridge. It bore his light weight easily, but when the giant reached the middle it broke, and he fell into the deep moat, and floundered there like a whale. Jack called for a rope, noosed the giant's heads, and drew them close to shore, so that he could cut them off with his sharp sword, and he sent the heads in a hired waggon, with six horses to draw it, as a little present to King Arthur.

Nothing ever seems to have happened to Jack except things that had to do with giants. In later years he won his wife from a giant and an enchanter who had changed her from a woman to a snow-white deer. She was the Count Palatine's daughter, and he was very much annoyed about it. And no one could rescue her, because she was in a magic castle guarded by sleepless griffins.

However, the coat of darkness made it easy to hood-wink the griffins, and Jack got safely to the castle gate. There hung a golden horn, with these words on it:

> *"Whoever can this trumpet blow*
> *Shall cause the giant's overthrow."*

"Come, that's simple," said Jack, and blew till he was out of breath.

And the gates flew open, and the castle fell into a heap of loose stones, crushing the giant and the magician. But the snow-white deer and a crowd of other enchanted creatures were unhurt, and as the dust of the falling castle settled down they found their own shapes again, and there was the Count Palatine's daughter, looking as pretty as a pink in June. The Count Palatine gave Jack her hand in marriage, which King Arthur said was the very least a grateful father could do. And the King himself added a handsome castle and a settled income, so that the pair were very well to do, and as happy as the day was long. Jack's father was sent for to Court, and well provided for.

Perhaps all the giants were dead, or perhaps Jack's wife thought he had killed enough giants for one man, or perhaps he was tired. At any rate, it is certain that after his marriage he killed no more giants.

PUSS IN BOOTS

THERE WAS ONCE a miller who had three sons, and all day they all worked in the mill, and were powdered white with the flour, that makes a sort of dun-coloured fog in mills, and at night they slept soundly because they had been working all day, and there is nothing like that to make you sleep like any old top. They used to get up very early in the morning, to get to work again. But the old miller was up earlier than any one. The four of them had saved enough money to keep the old man in comfort in the days when he should be too old for work, and they knew that by working as they had always done they could save enough to keep the three lads from the workhouse, or from having to beg, when they too should grow old. And they were all happy and contented. And then suddenly a dreadful thing happened. The miller lent all his money to a farmer friend, who promised to pay it back after harvest; but there was a flood, and the harvest was ruined. The farmer hanged himself to his own barn-beam, and the shock of losing at once his money and his friend was too much for the old miller, and he died. On his deathbed he said: "My dear sons, I leave the mill to Bertrand, who is the eldest, the donkey to Alain, my second son, and the mill cat to Yvo, my youngest, with my last blessing to you all."

So he died and was buried, and the two eldest brothers, with their mill and donkey, set to work to keep the trade going. But Yvo's cat was of no use in the mill except for mouse-catching, so Alain and Bertrand told him that he must look out for a home elsewhere.

Then they went off to cut sedge to mend the thatch-roof with, and Yvo was left alone with his cat, who sat looking at him with big round, yellow eyes.

"Much good you are to *me,* old fellow," he said to the cat. "You can catch mice and do pretty well for yourself— and that's a good thing. But the most you could do for me would be to die, and then I could make a cap out of your soft skin. And I'd rather you didn't die, so keep your life and enjoy it, old Michau, for I'm off to the wars for a soldier."

"Don't you be in such a hurry," said the cat. "Who told you I was only good for catching mice?"

"Eh?" said Yvo, who was as much astonished as you would be if your cat said anything more to you than "Miaow!" or "Purr."

"You're a good boy all the same," said the cat, licking his long white whiskers. "You don't wish me dead so as to have my skin, so I'll show you what I am good for. You go up into the back attic, where the beans and peas and roots are stored, and in the chink between the third and fourth boards close by the old cradle you'll find a tenpenny piece that has lain there this last hundred years. You take that to the shoemaker, and tell him to make me a pair of boots. Then you make me a bag—cut the tails of your shirt off if you haven't any other cloth—and run strings in the bag. Let me have them by Sunday, and then you shall see what you shall see."

Yvo did exactly as he was told, which was very sensible of him, and by Sunday the cat had his boots and his bag. The boots were beautiful boots—topboots with yellow heels—and the bag was made of the tails of Yvo's best blue shirt.

Very early on Monday morning Puss got up and went over the hill to a rabbit warren. The rabbits were out already nibbling the dewy grass; but the grass, though dewy, was short, and the rabbits were very hungry.

Michau laid out his bag, with parsley and bran in it, fixed the mouth of the bag open by a strong frond of bracken, and then hid himself behind a stone, holding the strings of the bag in his paws.

The silly bunnies saw and sniffed, and sniffed and longed, and longed and tasted, and two, bolder than the others, went head first into the bag, and plunged their greedy, nibbling noses right into the heap of bran.

That was what Puss had been waiting for. He pulled the strings, the strings drew up the mouth of the bag, and there were two fine fat rabbits kicking and struggling inside.

Michau killed each with a quick bite at the back of the neck, and then set out for the King's palace. When he got there he went to the side door, and asked to see the King, and all the handmaids and footmen and scullions and turn-spits laughed aloud at the very idea.

"*You* see the King?" said the cook; "you're much more likely to see the bottom of the moat, my fine fellow."

"Do you think so," said the cat. "I shouldn't be lonely there, anyhow—for you'd all be thrown after me as soon as the King knew that that was how you treated the messenger of my Lord the Marquis of Carabas."

"Oh, if you come from a marquis," said the cook, "that's quite a different pair of shoes. Raoul, show the gentleman up."

So one of the footmen who had been loudest in jeering at Michau had to lead him to the King's presence.

"A gift, your Majesty," said the cat, bowing low before the throne, "from your faithful servant my Lord the Marquis of Carabas."

"Why, I never heard of him," said the King. "But then it's true that I have not long moved into my present palace."

"Oh," said the cat carelessly, "my Lord Marquis owns a good deal of land not so very far away."

"Indeed," said the King.

"Thank your master, my fine cat, and be sure you don't leave the palace without a good meal."

Next day the cat caught a brace of partridges, and took them to the palace; next day it was pheasants. He always had a good meal before leaving, and the folks in the kitchen got to look for his coming, for Michau was the best of company, and could tell more stories, and more amusing ones, than any cat I ever heard of.

But Yvo said, "This is all very well for you—you are getting as fat as butter with all these free meals at the palace; but I get nothing but my brothers' leavings, and even those I shan't get much longer. They are growing tired of waiting for you to make my fortune."

"Don't you be so tiresome," said the cat. "All the time I'm eating I'm picking up bits of news from the servants, and presently I shall hear something that I can use to advance your fortunes. But if you worry I won't do anything at all—so there."

"Very well," said Yvo, "then I won't worry."

And the very next day, as the cat sat in the King's kitchen, happy in the good company of a venison pasty and a wooden bowl of cider, he heard news that made him swallow down the cider at one gulp, leave the best of the pasty, and run all the way home.

"Come along, master," the cat cried to Yvo, who was half asleep in the mill-house, "the King and the Princess Dulcibella are driving out in their coach today, and they are to go along by the river-side. So come quickly."

"It won't do me much good to see kings and princesses," said Yvo; but he followed the cat all the same.

And when they got to the river, that runs smooth and shallow between two rows of pollarded grey willows, the cat said:

"Now undress, and go into the water up to your neck. You're a pretty fellow enough; it's your clothes that spoil you, especially since you cut up your best blue shirt to make my game-bag."

The water was cold, and Yvo could not swim, but he did as Michau told him, and the cat put his clothes in the mouth of an otter's den, and kicked a turf in after them to hide them completely.

And in the water Yvo stayed, getting colder and colder and more and more uncomfortable, till the King's carriage came by. Then the cat stood up in his boots with the yellow heels, and put his paws to his mouth and shouted:

"Help, help! for my Lord Marquis of Carabas."

The King's carriage stopped, and the King put his head out to see what was the matter.

"My master was bathing," said the cat, "and some robbers came and carried off his clothes and his horse; and his castle is miles away, and he is in despair because he cannot come out of the water to greet your Majesty."

"Oh, is that all?" said the King; and he told his under-chamberlain to send a running footman back to the palace for a silver-laced suit, with hat, ruff, boots, and rapier, all complete. Then the carriage waited while Yvo came out of the water and dressed; and when he had on the fine suit he looked as fine a gentleman as anybody there. So he presented himself to the King, and the King presented him to the Princess, and he and she each thought they had never seen any one they liked so well.

"Let me give you a lift," said the King heartily, "and thank you for all the fine game you've been sending me lately. We're only going for a drive. I can drop you anywhere you like."

So Yvo, who had never before ridden in anything grander than a wheelbarrow, got into the coach with the King and the Princess. And Yvo and the Princess sat face to face; and, truth to tell, they found it hard to keep their eyes off each other.

The cat ran on ahead, till he came to a field where reapers were at work getting in a very fine harvest of corn.

"My men," he said, "if you do as I tell you you shall each have a pocketful of money. But if you don't my master will hang you. If the King asks you whose field this is you must say it belongs to the Lord Marquis of Carabas."

So when the King, who took an interest in farming, came to the field he admired the rich grain, and stopped his carriage to ask whose it was.

"It belongs to my Lord the Marquis of Carabas," said the reapers all together.

"Very fine indeed, my lord," said the King.

"It's the first good crop I've ever had from that field," said Yvo.

The cat hurried on to another field, where men were at work binding corn in sheaves, and spoke to them as he had done to the others. And when the King came along, and questioned them, they said with one voice:

"It all belongs to my Lord the Marquis of Carabas."

"Your estates are very large, my lord," said the King, "and very prosperous; I never saw a finer crop."

"It's almost a miracle," said Yvo, "for I never took any trouble with that field."

So the carriage drove on, and still the King looked at the corn-fields—and the Princess and Yvo looked at each other. And now the road left the river, and wound like a twisted white ribbon over the green velvet of smooth meadows to where, far off, at the foot of a hill, stood a large and beautiful castle.

"I wonder now whose that is?" said the King. "Let us go and see."

The cat took a very short cut across country, and got to the castle long before the King did. He had a little chat with the sentry at the keep, told him some funny tales, picked up a little gossip, and then went on to the castle itself, where he told the porter he had to deliver a message from his master the Marquis of Carabas.

Now this castle belonged to an ogre, and so did all the land for miles round. But if you think the cat was afraid of ogres you do not do him justice.

He went up to the great gate, pulled the great bell, and asked to see the master of the house; and his manners were so good and his language so fine that the porter led him into a great hall hung with beast-skins and furnished with old black oak. And there sat the ogre, as big as he was ugly, and as ugly as he was wicked.

"What do *you* want?" he asked the cat fiercely; and his mind was quite made up that, whatever the cat *wanted,* what the cat should get would be the end of a rope.

"Only to see *you,*" said the cat humbly; "and now I have seen you I can die contented."

"I'm not much to look at," said the ogre, but he was pleased all the same.

"Looks are not everything," said the cat, "though even in looks you are the finest ogre in all Brittany. I have travelled all over the world, in Europe, Asia, Africa, and the Island of Sark, and everywhere I have heard of nothing but your beauty, your wit, your wealth, and your accomplishments."

"Well," said the ogre, scratching his head, "you've got a tongue. Wet it with a cup of wine, and sit down and have a turnover or a girdle-cake."

"I'll sit down with pleasure," said Michau, "but I won't eat, thank you, because I've just had breakfast with the King, who owns the next-door kingdom to yours, and his lovely daughter, Princess Dulcibella."

"Oh," said the ogre, "and did *they* talk about me too?"

"I should think they did," said the cat. "They told me all I have told you, and more. Why, they said you had the power of changing yourself into any animal you chose; but of course, I'm not so mouse-minded as to believe *that.*"

"Oh, aren't you," said the ogre. "Well, then, look here." He stood up, took off his cloak, and said:

"I shall now change myself into a lion. No deception, ladies and gentlemen. You shall see for yourselves how it's done!"

He uttered a roar so loud that the other lions might almost have heard it in their distant deserts, and then and there became a lion. Michau was off through the window before the echo of the roar had died away. He landed on the sloping kitchen roof, but his boots made it very difficult to hold on to it, so he slid off, clattering on to the roof of the washhouse, and from that to the roof of the oven, and from that to the stones of the yard. And from the yard he ran in and upstairs, and peeped into the ogre's hall. The lion was gone, and only the ogre sat there, laughing all by himself at the fright he had given his visitor.

"Excuse my having left you for a moment," said the cat, walking in as though nothing had happened. "I thought I heard my master, the Marquis of Carabas, calling me. But it was only the well-handle creaking."

"You know well enough," said the ogre, "that you were frightened because I turned into a lion."

Michau smiled with polite amusement.

"Oh, not at all, I assure you," he said. "Why, that's such a common trick, if you'll pardon my saying so. Almost every one I know can do *that*. What the King was saying was that you could turn yourself into quite little things—a fly, or a beetle, or a mouse; and of course I'm not so bat-witted as to believe that."

"Oh, you aren't, aren't you?" said the ogre. "You just look here!" And with a squeak of triumph he turned himself into a mouse.

"Weet, weet!" said the ogre-mouse, frisking about under Michau's nose.

"Miaow!" said Michau, and pinned the ogre-mouse to the leg of the ogre's chair. There was no more ogre then; only a dead mouse, which Michau scorned to eat.

So that when the King and the Princess and Yvo arrived at the front door of the castle the cat had already been round to all the servants, explaining to them, as he had done to the reapers, that everything really belonged to the Marquis of Carabas; and the King was met by rows of bowing retainers, and by Michau, who came to meet the coach, saying:

"Welcome, your Majesty, to the halls of the most noble the Marquis of Carabas."

"So this is your country seat, is it?" said the King. "Sly dog, not to say a word when we were wondering whose this fine estate could be!"

"Enter, your Majesty," said Yvo, "and let us see if my major-domo can find a crust to set before you."

The cat hurried away, and ordered a banquet to be served as soon as possible. The King was so pleased with looking at the castle gardens and pleasaunces that dinner seemed ready in no time. And it was a dinner fit for any king. As for the new Marquis of Carabas and the Princess, they had eyes for nothing but each other.

The King, who had eyes for everything, saw this, and when his wine cup was filled for the seventh time he raised it so that its jewels flashed in the afternoon sun, and said, winking at the cat, who stood beside Yvo's chair:

"I cannot help thinking that the noble Marquis is worthy by his person and his estates of my daughter's hand, and I am sure no one who has seen them together can doubt what they think about it. Bless you, my children! To the health of Princess Dulcibella and the Marquis of Carabas!"

The King feasted three days in the castle of the Marquis of Carabas, and then the young people were married. The two brothers were invited, but they were too shy to come, so Yvo made one of them his wood-reeve and the other his grand almoner, and everyone was quite happy, especially Michau, whose cleverness had brought all this happiness about; because making other people happy is really astonishingly pleasant, as you will find if you try it.

Of course, Michau told a lot of stories, but then all's fair when you're dealing with ogres.

JACK AND THE BEANSTALK

JACK LIVED WITH his mother in a little cottage. It had dormer windows and green shutters whose hinges were so rusty that the shutters wouldn't shut. Jack had taken some of them to make a raft with. He was always trying to make things that seemed like the things in books—rafts or sledges, or wooden spear-heads to play at savages with, or paper crowns with which to play at kings. He never did any work; and this was very hard on his mother, who took in washing, and had great trouble to make both ends meet. But he did not run away to sea, or set out to seek his fortune, because he knew that that would have broken his mother's heart, and he was very fond of her. Though he wouldn't work, he did useless pretty things for her— brought her bunches of wild-flowers, and made up songs, sad and merry, and sang them to her of an evening. But most of the time he spent in looking at the sky and the clouds and the green leaves and the running water, and thinking how beautiful the world was, and how he would love to see every single thing in it. And he always seemed to be trying to dream one particular dream, and never could quite dream it. Sometimes the thought of his mother working so hard while he did nothing would come suddenly upon him, and he would rush off and try to help her, but whatever he did turned out wrong. If he went to draw water he was sure to lose the bucket in the well; if he lifted the wash-tub it always slipped out of his fingers, and then

48

there was the floor to clean as well as the linen to wash all over again. So that it always ended in his mother saying. "Oh, run along, for goodness' sake, and let me get on with my work." And then Jack would go and lie on his front and look at the ants busy among the grass stalks, and make up a pretty poem about the Dignity of Labour, or about how dear and good mothers were.

But poetry, however pretty, is difficult to sell, and the two got poorer and poorer. And at last one day Jack's mother came out to where he was lying on his back watching the clouds go sailing by, and told him that the worst had come.

"No help for it," she said; "we must sell the cow."

"Oh, let me take it to market," cried Jack, jumping up. "I shall pretend to myself I'm a rich farmer with a cow to sell every market-day."

So the rope halter, with Jack at one end of it and the cow at the other, started off down the road.

"Ask five gold pieces for her," said the Mother, "and take what you can get; and don't let the grass grow under your feet."

Jack went along very slowly, and kept his eyes fixed to the ground, because if the grass *did* grow under his feet he wanted to watch it growing. So this was how it was that he ran plump into something hard, and, looking up, saw a butcher, very smart in a new blue coat with a red carnation in his button-hole.

"Who are you shoving of, young shaver?" the butcher asked crossly. "Why don't you look where you're going?"

"Because I thought I might see you," said Jack.

"Ha! I see you're a clever boy," said the butcher, not at all offended. "Thinking of selling your cow?"

"Well," said Jack, "that was rather the idea."

"And what's the price?"

"Five gold pieces," said Jack boldly.

"I wouldn't rob you of her by offering such a poor price," said the butcher kindly. "Look here."

He pulled out a handful of large, bright-coloured beans.
"Aren't they beautiful?" he said.

"Oh, they are—they are!" said Jack. And they were.
They had all the colours and all the splendour of precious
stones.

"I never saw anything at all like them," said Jack, and
longed to have them in his pockets, to take them out and
play with them whenever he liked.

"Well, is it a bargain?" the butcher asked.

"Oh, yes," said Jack. "Take the ugly old cow."

And with that he took the beans, thrust the end of the
rope into the butcher's hand, and hurried off towards
home.

I don't think I had better tell you what happened when
he told his mother what he had done. You can perhaps
guess. I will only say that it ended in his mother throwing
the beans out of the window and sending Jack to bed
without his supper. Then she spent the evening ironing,
and every now and then a tear fell down and hissed and
fizzled on the hot iron.

The next morning Jack woke up feeling very hot and
half choked. He found his room rather darker than usual,
and at first he decided that it was too early to get up; then
as he was just snuggling the blanket closer round his neck
he saw what it was that was shutting out the sunshine.
The beans had grown up into a huge twisted stalk with
immense leaves. When Jack ran to the window and
pushed his hand out among the green he could see no top
to the plant. It seemed to grow right up into the sky. Then
suddenly Jack was a changed boy. Something wonderful
had happened to him, and it had made him different. It
sometimes happens to people that they see or hear something quite wonderful, and then they are never altogether
the same again.

Jack scrambled into his clothes, ran to the door, and
shouted:

"Mother, those beautiful beans have grown! I told you
I'd made a good bargain with that silly old cow. I'm going

to climb up and see what's at the top." And before his mother could stop him he was out of the window and up the beanstalk, climbing and wriggling among the branches, and when she reached the window he was almost out of sight. She stood looking up after him till she couldn't see him any more, and then she sighed, and went up to her son's untidy room, to make his bed and set all straight for him.

Jack climbed on and on until his head felt dizzy and his legs and arms ached. He had had no supper last night, you remember, and no breakfast before he started. But at last there was no more stalk to climb, and as soon as he reached the top tendril it suddenly flattened and opened out before him into a long white dusty road. He was in a new land, and as far as he could see nothing else was alive in that land but himself. The trees were withered, the fields were bare, and every stream had run dry. Altogether it was not at all a nice place; but if it wasn't nice it was new; and besides, he could not face the idea of going down that beanstalk again without anything to eat, and he set out to look for a house and beg a breakfast. At that moment something dark came between him and the light—fluttered above his head, and then settled on the road beside him.

"Oh, mercy! I thought it was a great bird," cried Jack. But it wasn't. It was a fairy—Jack knew that at once, though he had never seen one before. There are some things you cannot mistake.

"Well, Jack," said the fairy, "I've been looking for you."

"I believe I've been looking for you all my life, if you come to that," said Jack.

"Yes, you have," said the fairy. "Now listen."

She told Jack a story that made him all hot, and cold, and ashamed, and eager to do something heroic at once, for she explained how the new land he had found had once belonged to his father, who was a good and great man, and who had ruled his land well and been loved by his subjects. But unfortunately one of his subjects happened to be a giant, and, being naturally of a large size, he considered himself more important than anyone else, and he had killed Jack's father, and with the help of a bad fairy had imprisoned the faithful subjects in the trees. Since the giant's rule began the land had not flourished—nothing would grow on it, the houses fell down in ruins and the waters ran dry. So the giant had shut himself and his wife up in a large white house with his precious belongings, and there he lived his selfish, horrid life.

"Now," said the fairy, "the time has come for you to set things straight. And this is really what you've been trying to dream about all your life. You must find the giant and get back your father's land for your mother. She has worked for you all your life. Now you will work for her; but you have the best of it, because her work was mending and washing and cooking and scrubbing, and your work is—adventures. Go straight on and do the things that first come into your head. This is good advice in ordinary life, and it works well in this land too. Good-bye."

And with a flutter of sea-green, shining wings the fairy vanished, and Jack was left staring into nothingness. He didn't stare long though, for, as I said before, he was a changed boy. There are plenty of people who could go in for adventures splendidly, but somehow they are never able to do anything else, and if they don't happen to fall in with adventures they can do nothing but dream of them, and so have a poor time of it in this world. Jack was one of these people. Only he, you see, had got out of this world and had fallen in with adventures into the bargain.

He went along the road, and when he came to a large white house the first thing he thought of doing was, curiously enough, to knock at the door and ask for something to eat, just as you or I would have done if we had gone up a large beanstalk without our breakfast or our last night's supper.

"Go away!" said the little old woman who opened the door, just as many people do if you ask them for something to eat and they don't happen to know you. "My husband is a giant, and he'll eat you if he sees you."

"You needn't let him see me," said Jack. "I haven't had anything to eat for *ages*. Do give me something, there's a good sort!"

So she took him in and gave him some bread and butter and a poached egg, and before he was half-way through it the whole house began to shake, and the old woman seized Jack, put his eggy plate into his hand, and pushed him into the oven and closed the door.

Jack had the sense not to call out, and he finished his egg in the oven. Then he found he could see through the crack near the hinges, so he glued his eye to it and saw! He saw the giant—a great big fat man with red hair and mutton-chop whiskers. The giant flung himself down at the table and roared for his dinner, and his trembling old wife brought him a whole hog, which he tore in pieces in his hands and ate without any manners, and he didn't offer his wife so much as a piece of the crackling. When he had finished he licked his great greasy fingers and called out: "Bring me my hen!"

Jack was rather surprised. He thought it was a curious creature to have on the dinner-table. But the next instant he understood, for the hen stood on the table, and every time the giant said "Lay!" it laid a golden egg.

It went on doing this until Jack thought it must be really tired, and until the giant *was*, for he lay back in his chair and fell asleep.

The first thing that occurred to Jack to do was to leap out of the oven, seize the hen under his arm, and make off for the beanstalk and his home as fast as ever he could.

I won't describe the scene in the cottage when he arrived. His mother was inclined to scold him, but when she thoroughly understood about the hen she kissed him instead, and said that she had always believed he would do something clever, some day.

Jack sold golden eggs at the market every week, and his mother gave up taking in washing; but she still went on

cleaning the cottage herself. I believe she rather liked that
kind of work.

Then suddenly one morning, as Jack stood in the cottage garden with his hands in the pockets of a quite new
pair of lavender-coloured breeches, he felt he couldn't go
on living without another journey up the beanstalk, and
forgetting to tell his mother that he might not be in to
dinner, he was off and up. He found the same dry, withered land at the top, and, although he was not hungry this
time, he couldn't think of anything new to say, so he said
the same thing to the old woman; but this time he found
it much harder to get round her, although she did not
know him again. Either his face was changed, or the lavender-coloured breeches were a complete disguise.

"No," she kept on saying, and Jack lost his temper when
she had said it twenty-two times. "A boy came before, and
he was a bad one and a thief, and I can't let another boy
in."

"But I've got an honest face," said Jack. "Everybody
says so."

"That's true," said the woman, and she let him in. This
time he was obliged to hide before he had begun to eat,
and he was rather glad, because, as I said, he was not
hungry—the giant's wife had only given him bread and
cheese, and the cheese was rather stale. When they heard
the giant coming along the road the woman lifted the copper lid and made Jack get in.

The giant seemed in a good temper, for he chucked his
wife under the chin and said:

"Fresh meat today, my dear. I can smell it."

"I'm—I'm afraid you're wrong," said his wife; and Jack
could hear by the way she said it that she was very frightened. "It's half the ox you had yesterday, and that fresh
meat you smell is just a bit of a dead cart-horse that a
crow dropped on the roof."

The giant seemed sulky after that, and didn't eat his
dinner with much appetite, and when his wife was clearing away he suddenly laid hold of her and shouted:

"Bring me my money-bags!"

Jack couldn't help lifting up the copper lid a little bit when he heard the chink of the coins, and when he saw the giant counting out the great heap of gold and silver he longed to have it for his own, for he knew that it ought by rights to belong to him or his mother.

Presently the giant fell asleep, and Jack looked all round to see if the wife was about before he dared to get out of the copper. And he heard her walking about upstairs, so he jumped out, seized on the bags, and again made off for the beanstalk.

He reached home as his mother was clearing away the dinner-plates; but I won't describe the scene. Of course they were now rich, and Jack wished to live in a large house, but his mother said she couldn't leave the "bits of things," and when he came to think it over Jack felt that he couldn't bear to leave the beanstalk.

Another day came when Jack felt he must make another journey to the giant's land, disguised in a new smock-frock and gaiters, and again the same thing happened, except that it was harder than ever to persuade the giant's wife to take him in. She did at last, however, after explaining that two boys had served her badly, and that if he turned out bad too, then the giant would most likely kill her.

No sooner was Jack inside the house than the giant was heard coming. The woman showed Jack an empty barrel, and he crept under it.

Then the giant came in, and he rolled his eyes, twisted his great head about, and swore that he smelt fresh meat. His wife told him he was wrong, but this time he didn't believe her, and he looked in the copper and in the oven and in the bread-crock, and under the sink; but he never thought of the empty barrel—partly, I daresay, because he thought it was full of something that it wasn't full of.

At last he gave up the search and sat down to his dinner, and when he had finished he stretched himself until Jack thought some of his buttons would burst, and called:

"Wife, bring me my harp!"

The old woman brought in a beautiful golden harp, which she set on the table, and as soon as the giant said, "Play!" it began to give out beautiful soothing music, and the giant presently fell asleep, while his wife went into the back kitchen to wash up.

The first thing that occurred to Jack was to upset the barrel, dash to the table, and take the harp, but as his hands touched it it cried out in a human voice, "Master, master!" For one second Jack nearly dropped it; then he realised that the giant was waking. He rushed to the door, kicking the cat in his hurry as he heard the giant stumble out after him. But the giant was heavy and only half awake, and by the time Jack was down the beanstalk the giant was only just at the top; but he was coming down, that was quite plain, for the next moment the great beanstalk shook and shivered with his great weight. Jack screamed to his mother for a chopper, and, like the good woman she was, she brought it without asking what it was for. Jack hacked at the beanstalk, and it cut like butter, so that when it fell the giant fell down with it and was killed, and that was the end of him.

And now Jack and his mother had plenty to live upon, and might have rented a palace if they had liked, but still Jack's mother wouldn't leave her cottage. As for the enchanted land up above—well, the fairy told Jack that after the death of the giant the people came out of the trees, and the land flourished under the rule of the giant's wife, a most worthy woman, whose only fault was that she was too ready to trust boys.

DICK WHITTINGTON AND HIS CAT

WHEN DICK WHITTINGTON'S father and mother died he was still only a little boy, and he had no relations to take care of him. All the neighbours were poor too, so that they could not afford to give him more than just odds and ends of things to eat, and odds and ends of clothes to wear. He had nowhere to sleep at all, except under a hay-stack or a hedge; and though that is very pleasant on hot summer nights, it is very horrid at any other time of the year.

Poor Dick was too young to be much good at hard work. But he always kept on saying to himself, "Never mind; when I'm a little bit older I shall get work, and be paid for it, and grow rich, and be perfectly happy." Like every other little boy in the world, he was always dreaming of what he would do when he grew up; and there was one word that came over and over again in his thoughts, and round it gathered all his dreams of riches and beauty. That word was "London." You see, nobody he knew really well had ever been there; for Dick lived a long time ago, hundreds of years before there were railway trains and motor-cars or even those jolly post-chaises that you see pictures of, with coachmen in white hats and somebody behind blowing a horn. In Dick's time, if people wanted to go anywhere they had to ride on horseback; and if they were too poor to have horses, as all Dick's friends were, then they had to walk; so of course it was quite impossible to go gaily off to London for the weekend, and nobody ever went so far except those who had business there and meant to stay a long time.

Now Dick, having no work to keep him busy, used to spend a lot of his time loitering near the water-trough in the village, because the folk who were going on journeys to and from London used to stop there for their horses to drink, and then if they noticed Dick they would some-times pass the time of day with him, and make jokes. If they looked really kind, he would summon up courage to ask them about where they had been, and what the great world was like out beyond the place where the white road was cut off short by the sky; and the stories they told him were different according to the sort of people they were. Some just said the simple truth, and that is often dull; but some, who liked to see his childish eyes grow big and round with wonder, made up the most wonderful tales about their adventures; and the most wonderful things of all were the things he heard about London Town. There, he was told, the streets were paved with red gold, and the houses roofed with tiles of silver, and there were always bells making music and flags fluttering, yellow and green and purple and blue; and all the people were big and beautiful, and honest and kind and happy.

The more he heard of London the more he dreamt of it by day and by night, until it seemed to him that the only thing in the whole world worth doing was to go there at once, and live there for always, and be big and beautiful and all the other nice things himself. But it seemed dread-fully far away, and there might be nobody along the road generous enough to give him food; and he was young and weak, and what could he do? So it went on for a long time—hunger and poverty for poor Dick, with nothing but his dreams of London Town to give him happiness.

But at last it happened—as things always do happen if only you wait long enough—that a lucky chance of actu-ally going to London fell in Dick's way. And this was how it was. A waggon went lumbering by, with the friendliest-looking waggoner you ever saw walking beside it and cracking a big whip. Just as they passed Dick a heavy sack fell off the waggon, and the man called out in a very jovial voice, "Come here and help me hoist this up, and I'll give you a ride as far as you like to go." So Dick helped him as well as he could, and when they had got the sack up again he said to the waggoner:

"Please, where are you going with your cart and horse?"

And the waggoner answered: "To London, my inquisitive child."

Then Dick's heart began to beat like a hammer, and he seemed to see all in a moment the coloured flags fluttering, and the golden streets shining, and the silver tiles flashing in the sun; and he seemed to hear the innumerable bells of a great city all ringing in harmony and making the most beautiful music in the world. Tears came into his eyes, and he clasped his hands.

"Oh do, *do* take me to London with you!" he cried. "I can't tell you how much I want to go." And the waggoner kept his word, and gave him a ride as far as he liked, which, of course, was the whole way to London; only it took them a great many days, and they had to run the risk of robbers on the journey, and so they had good reason to be glad when at last they were safely there. Dick did not feel glad at all. For he looked round and round and round, and nowhere at all could he see the golden pavement or the silver tiles; and there wasn't a single bell ringing the whole town through.

Now the waggoner, though he was kind and honest, was rather stupid, and when he saw Dick almost in tears, and not a bit pleased to have come safely through so long a journey, he thought him most ungrateful, and packed him off without listening to a word of explanation.

So there was Dick without a friend and without a penny; and, for all his bitter disappointment, he knew that he must set out at once to find work or he would starve. So, like a brave boy, he wasted no time, but began to look about him. Even for a big strong man work is often terribly hard to find, and Dick could think of nothing that he might turn his hand to.

For a long time he had to get on as best he could by odd jobs, and once he was lucky enough to be given some haymaking to do in Holborn. I know that doesn't sound right, because those of you who have been to Holborn think of offices and bicycle-shops and hotels, all sorts of great buildings, and omnibuses and cabs and men in tophats; but in Dick's time, though you never would think it, most of London was still green and countrified; and Dick made hay in Holborn all those hundreds of years ago, which is rather strange to think of.

But the haymaking season passed, and the cold weather came on, and Dick began to have bad luck; till one night when he had had no food for two days he lay down in despair and went to sleep on a doorstep that happened to be handy. And on this doorstep the owner of the house, a merchant whose name was Fitzwarren, found him in the morning.

"Get up," said Master Fitzwarren, quite kindly. And when Dick had got up he went on:

"How is it you are not at work and earning your living?"

"Indeed, sir," said Dick, "I should be very glad of the chance."

And, seeing that he meant it, Master Fitzwarren took him indoors and gave him soup and pudding, and engaged him straight away as a scullery-boy.

Now he would have been happy enough if it had not been for the cook. She was a disagreeable old thing, and having some one under her, she liked to show her power, so she showed it by tormenting Dick in every possible way. Some people are like that. When they are Czars or Kings we call them tyrants; when they are cooks we call them—but let us be polite, whatever we are! The head footman, however, took a fancy to Dick, and gave him little presents of sweets and toys, and also—which was far the best and kindest thing he could have done—taught him to read.

Also Master Fitzwarren had a daughter, named Alice; and she too was kind to Dick; so that he was not as badly off as he might have been. Still, his life was very sad; he was continually in trouble with the cook, and he did not see any chance of ever being more than a scullery-boy.

One day, however, something happened which was to turn out the most important event in his life, though, of course, he did not know it at the time. Miss Alice sent him to the bleaching-ground to fetch home some linen; and there he saw the spurrier's little daughter, Madge, feeding a cat with milk out of a platter. Dick looked at the cat, and longed to have it for his own. He had in his pocket a silver groat (or fourpenny-bit) which an alderman had given him for cleaning his shoes. So he went up to Madge and said:

"Please will you sell me that cat? How much is it?"

"Why," said the little girl, "my brother was going to drown it this morning, only I saved it; and now I wish I could find some one to take it and be good to it, for to be sure I don't know what to do with it myself."

"Take my groat," said Dick, "and give me the cat"

"No," answered Madge, "I will not take your money; but you may have the cat if you give me that bunch of roses in your cap."

That, then, was how Dick got his famous cat; and now you will see why I said this was the most important thing that ever happened to him; for quite a short time after-wards Master Fitzwarren called all his servants together, and said to them:

"I am sending out one of my ships to trade in a far coun-try, and if each of you will give me something of your own I will tell the captain to exchange it with the merchants of that country, and bring back to you whatever he gets for it."

All the servants were delighted at this chance of making a little money, and every one of them brought something to be traded with except poor Dick, who had not a penny in the world, and no belongings except the clothes he wore and—*his cat.*

"Please," he said, very sorrowfully, "I have nothing of my own except a cat, and I suppose that is no good to anybody."

But Master Fitzwarren thought it would be a good joke to send the cat and see what could be got for it, so he laughed and told Dick to bring it along; and Dick fetched pussy, though he felt sad at parting from her. And the captain and the cat sailed away down the Thames and out over the blue sea, and Dick made up his mind it was no good thinking about that business any more, and went back to his drudgery in the kitchen.

But there things gradually got worse and worse; for the cook had noticed that Miss Alice was kind to the boy, and she was jealous; so she managed to set all the other servants against him, and he got nothing but kicks and blows the whole day long, till at last he felt he could bear it no longer. So one morning, very early indeed, he tied up his clothes in a handkerchief, and crept out silently, and made off towards Highgate. You can go to Highgate now in a motor-bus or an underground tube, whichever you like, but Dick had only one way of going, and that was on his two legs, so that presently he began to be tired, and sat down on a stone to rest. And that stone to this day is called "Whittington's Stone." Suddenly as he sat there the bells of Bow Church in Cheapside began to ring; and as their chimes were borne to him on the still, clear air of early morning there came up before his mind his old dream of London as a city of silver and gold and flags and sweet-sounding bells, and it seemed to him that there was a mist before his eyes, and the bells seemed to come from a great way off, and to have words fitted to the tune of them. What they sang was this:

"Turn again, Whittington!
Whittington, turn again!
Turn again, Whittington,
Lord Mayor of London!"

And he believed the bells, and got up from the stone, and ran home as fast as he could, and was back in the kitchen at Master Fitzwarren's before the cook came down— which was very lucky for him, as is plain if you consider what was meanwhile happening to the ship that had gone on its voyage, and to the captain, and the cat. For the ship, which was trying to get to Italy, was caught in a storm, and lost its bearings. The rain blinded the sailors, and the waves washed over their decks, and a great wind blew and blew and blew till it landed them high and dry on a big bank of sand. When the storm died away and they could look about them they saw that the natives of the place, who came down to them, were Moors; and the captain, who had once travelled in Asia, talked to one of the chiefs of these natives in Arabic, and, very fortunately, found that he was understood.

Now the name of this place was Barbary. The Moors were kind and hospitable to the shipwrecked mariners, and willing to give them all sorts of precious merchandise in exchange for the knives and scissors and other things they had brought from England. Moreover, the King of Barbary himself entertained the captain at a great banquet, where all the dishes were of gold and silver and clear crystal, and all the foods and drinks more delicious than anything you ever had even at a birthday party.

But—a strange and terrible thing came to pass, which astonished the captain beyond measure. As soon as ever the servants began to bring in the food and set it before the guests hundreds of rats and mice darted out from every quarter of the room, and splashed in the gravy and gnawed the food and spoilt the whole delightful feast. The

King, nearly crying with vexation, turned to the captain and exclaimed:

"This has been the worry of my life ever since I and my people came to this country. We have tried everything we can think of, and none is any good. I would give untold treasure to the man who should rid me of this plague."

Of course the captain thought at once of Dick Whittington's cat; and he said to the King:

"If you will allow me to send to my ship, I think I can show you a beast that will put an end to your troubles by killing the rats and mice."

The King was overjoyed to hear this, and ordered a strong bodyguard to go to the ship for the cat; for he fancied that a beast which could destroy his enemies must be very great and terrible indeed.

You can imagine his surprise when the soft, sleek, purring pussy-cat was brought before him.

"Can this amiable animal really assist us?" he asked.

"You shall see," said the captain.

He asked that a new banquet should be spread, and as soon as it appeared out came the rats and the mice in their hundreds, waggling their whiskers and their tails; and down on them came the cat, all teeth and claws, and killed and killed and killed until the floor was covered with the dead, and all the rats and mice that weren't dead had run away. Then the King was as good as his word, and bought the cat for plates of gold and bars of silver, heaps of woven cloths, and boxes upon boxes of precious stones. And of course all these belonged to Dick Whittington, because he had been promised that he should have whatever price his cat might bring.

So when the captain, after a safe voyage home, had told the whole wonderful story to Master Fitzwarren, Dick was sent for and told the splendid story of his cat's success. And he ceased to be a scullery-boy, and became rich and important all in a moment. The news took his breath away and left him speechless with joy.

But gradually as the days went by he began to get accustomed to the change, and to plan what he would do with all his wealth; and I will tell you two of the things he did. One of them, of course, was to marry Miss Alice, whom he had worshipped all the years that he was only a poor scullery-boy; and the other, which did not happen till after many years of work, and thought, and good deeds, when he was a great merchant, was to become Lord Mayor of London, just as the bells had told him he would. And he was Lord Mayor not only once, but three times; and he did good, and cared for the poor, and built a hospital and an almshouse, and took thought how he might lessen all the poverty he saw round him; for he remembered what it was like to be penniless, and hungry, and out of work, and to find that the streets were not paved with gold nor the houses roofed with silver. And if only people who are rich now thought half as much as he did about the poor, what a much pleasanter place the world would be!

THE SLEEPING BEAUTY IN THE WOOD

WHENEVER YOU GIVE a christening party you must always remember to ask all the most disagreeable people you know. It is very dangerous to neglect this simple precaution. Nearly all the misfortunes which happen to princesses come from their relations having forgotten to invite some nasty old fairy or other to their christenings. This was what happened in the case of the Sleeping Beauty.

She was not called the Sleeping Beauty at her christening, of course; for though she was certainly a beauty even then, she did not sleep more than any other little baby. She was called Benevola, after the most powerful of the seven good fairies who were invited to her christening. And because one name is never enough for a princess, she had six other names, which were the names of the other six fairies.

It was a charming christening party. The Queen had never had a baby of her own before, and she wished the christening party to be one of those parties that people remember and talk of for a long time afterwards. Well, she had her wish; for though this all happened hundreds of years ago, that party has never been forgotten—and here we are talking about it now!

The Queen insisted that the party should not be given in the town palace, but in the beautiful country palace where the Court usually spent the summer. It was a lovely place,

66

with gardens and terraces, and peacocks, and fountains and goldfish; and all round it was a park, and round the park was a wood, and the palace itself was old and grey and beautiful, with big towers like beer-mugs, and little turrets like pepper-pots, and a dovecot like a great round cheese with holes in it, and a lawn in the courtyard that was like a green velvet table-cover.

And here the christening feast was given. Everything was pink and white. The walls were hung with white satin looped up with festoons of pink roses; the Queen wore a white dress and a pink velvet mantle; the baby had white cambric robes tied up at the sleeves with pink ribbon (because it was a girl; if it had been a boy the ribbons would have had to be blue, and I don't know how the Court decorators would have managed about the roses, for blue roses are very uncommon). There were strawberry and lemon ices—pink and white—and pink and white blancmange; and the christening cake was covered with white icing, with "Benevola! Bless her!" on it in pink letters; and the very tablecloths were white, and the very toes of the baby the prettiest pink you ever saw.

After dinner the fairies all gave their christening presents to the little Princess, beginning with the youngest. They gave her beauty and grace, and wit and loving-kindness, and the sense of humour, and the sense of honour. What princess could wish for more?

"And now, Benevola dear," said the happy mother Queen, turning to the eldest good fairy, "I'm just dying to know what your present is. I know it'll be something perfectly lovely. *Oh!*"

The last word was nearly a scream; and every one else screamed too, though, as a rule, screaming is not allowed at Court. But on an occasion like this no one was shocked. It was, people agreed afterwards, enough to make anybody scream. For quite suddenly, with a clap of thunder and a nasty flash of forked lightning, the fairy Malevola dropped through the ceiling, and stood with her ugly flat feet firmly planted on the white and pink rose-leaves that were heaped round the baby's cradle.

"How do you do?" said the King, breaking the dreadful silence.

"So pleased you were able to come," twittered the Queen. "Most kind of you to drop in like this."

Malevola scowled and spoke. "You didn't ask me to this christening party."

The King murmured something about having lost her address.

"You never looked for my address; you didn't want my address. You didn't ask me to your party. No one ever does ask me to their parties."

"And I don't wonder," whispered the youngest lady-in-waiting. Malevola, indeed, did not look exactly the sort of person to be the life and soul of a party. She had a cruel, ugly, yellow face, shiny bat's wings, which she pretended were a fashionable cloak, and a bonnet trimmed with live snakes. Her scarf was tied together with a bunch of earthworms, and she wore a live toad for a brooch.

"However," she went on, "I'm not offended. I've brought your dear daughter a little present."

"Now that's really charming of you," said the poor Queen, looking round for Benevola. But Benevola had disappeared.

"*Such* a nice present," said the wicked fairy. "Benevola you've called her, have you? Sweet little pet! Well, Benevola darling, you shall prick your hand with a spindle and die of the wound. *Won't* that be nice?"

And with that, and another clap of thunder, Malevola vanished.

The Queen caught up the baby, and Benevola crept cautiously out from behind the white velvet window curtains.

"Is she gone?" she asked. "Cheer up, dear Queen. I'm glad I kept my gift to the last."

"Then you can undo Malevola's wicked work," cried the Queen, smiling through her tears.

"No, not that; but I can change it. My little goddaughter must prick her hand with a spindle, but she shall not die of it. She shall only sleep for a hundred years."

"That's just as bad for me," said the Queen, hugging her baby.

"Not quite, dear," said Benevola kindly. "You'll see."

"In the meantime," said the King, who had been very busy with his tablets, "Heaven helps those who help themselves. I've made a new law. Shall I recite it?"

"Oh, do, your Majesty!" said everybody; and the youngest lady-in-waiting whispered, "His Majesty does write such sweet, pretty laws."

"The law is," said the King, "'No spindles allowed in my kingdom, on pain of death.'"

Every one clapped their hands, and the Queen dried her eyes and kissed the baby.

Princess Benevola grew up a perfect dear, and her parents loved her more and more, and when she asked if she mightn't keep her eighteenth birthday at the country palace they saw no reason why she shouldn't.

That business of Malevola had almost been forgotten. No spindles were ever seen in that country, and where there are no spindles it is impossible to prick yourself with them.

So the birthday party was given in the same hall that had been hung with white and pink for the christening party, and now the festoons of roses were red and white, and pink and yellow; "For," said Benevola, "I love them all."

On the day after the party the Princess explored the castle, and she and her maids had a good game of hide-and-seek. When it was the Princess's turn to hide she thought it would be amusing to hide in one of the little round turrets that were like pepper-pots. So she opened the door of one, and there sat an old woman doing something so interesting that the Princess at once forgot all about the hide-and-seek.

"What are you doing, good dame?" the Princess asked.

"Spinning flax, child," said the old woman. And she was—the shining, polished spindle twirled round and round in her fingers.

"It's pretty work," said the Princess. "Do you think I could do it?"

"You can try, and welcome," said the old woman. "Sit in my chair, and take the spindle in your hand."

Benevola did as she was told; but as she sat down one pointed end of the spindle knocked against the arm of the chair, and the other pointed end ran into the palm of her hand. The blood started out on her white gown, and Benevola fell to the ground in a swoon.

"Ha, ha!" said the old woman, and turned into Malevola before the Princess's eyes (only those eyes were shut). "Ha, ha! Your father never thought how easily I could make a spindle when the time came." And with that and the usual clap of thunder she vanished.

And so when the Princess's ladies burst into the room in their game of hide-and-seek, all laughing and chattering like a cageful of bright-coloured parrots, they found the Princess lying flat on the floor, as white as a snowdrop and as still as death.

The ladies ran screaming to tell the King and Queen, and when they climbed the turret stairs and lifted their dear lifeless daughter between them the spindle fell out of the folds of her dress and rattled and spun on the bare floor.

So then they knew.

"Send for Benevola," moaned the Queen. "Oh, send for Benevola—do!" And the King tried to drown his grief by giving orders about the bed his child was to lie on during her long sleep, as many another father has done before and since.

They laid the white Princess on a bed of carved ebony hung with curtains of silver cloth, and over her body they laid a coverlet of cloth of gold that fell to the ground on both sides in folds that looked like folds carved in the solid metal. And they put a pink rose and a white rose and a yellow rose on her breast, and crossed her hands above them; and over all they laid a veil of white gauze that covered her from head to feet, and they shut the door and went away and left her.

And then Benevola came. The poor Queen rushed down the throne steps and along the great hall to meet her, and—

"Oh, my girl!" she cried. "Oh, my pretty little baby! She will sleep for a hundred years, and I shall be dead long, long years before she wakes up, and I shall never see her pretty eyes or her dear smile or hear her call me mother ever again."

And with that she broke once more into wild weeping. Benevola put her arms round the Queen's neck and kissed her.

"You poor dear!" she said. "Don't grieve so. Your daughter must sleep for a hundred years. But what of that? *So shall you.* Yes, and the King her father, and all the courtiers and waiting-maids, and knights and men-at-arms— and the very dogs and cats. And when she wakes you shall all waken too, and, in the light of the happiness you will know when you feel her loving arms round you again all this present sorrow will be to you as a dream is when one wakes to see the brave sun shining."

"You are sure she *will* wake?" said the mother Queen, clinging to her.

"When the hundred years are over a prince shall come and wake her," said the fairy. "He will love her very much, and he shall be her husband."

"Then I shall lose her anyway," sighed the Queen.

"That's what mothers are born to," said the fairy. "Come, eat and drink a little, all of you, before you go to sleep."

So the tables were set, and every one ate and drank, though it was with a heavy heart. And as the dinner was drawing to an end the fairy suddenly spoke the spell, and everyone in the palace fell asleep in his place. The King and Queen at the high table, the page filling the wine cup, the butler carrying fruit on a salver, the servants cleaning pots in the kitchen, the huntsman feeding his hounds, the hounds leaping round him, the cat basking on the terrace, the pigeons cuddled on the roof tiles—all were struck into sleep just as they were, so that the palace looked as though it were peopled with waxworks instead of living folk.

The fairy sighed and smiled, and sighed again. Then she laid a spell on the place so that no dust or decay should come near it in those hundred long years. And she laid a spell on the gardens, that no weeds should grow, and that all the flowers should stay just as they were, to the last least leaf or bud. The wood, too, she laid a spell on, and at once the branches grew thick and many, the briars and creepers wound in and out among the branches, and in a moment there was a thicket round the garden as tough and unpassable as any old quickset hedge.

There was one more spell to lay, and Benevola laid it. It was on the people, so that they should not seek to find or to bring back their King and Queen. She laid a spell to make them all Republicans for a hundred years, when they should become loyal again the moment the King awoke—which was really quite a good idea, and met every possible difficulty.

So a year went by, and the seasons changed the face of the country from brown to green, and from green to yellow, and from yellow to russet, and from russet to white. But in the garden within the ring of the wood nothing changed at all. There it was always high midsummer, and the roses flamed in the sunshine, and the jasmine flowers shone like stars in the twilight. And the years went on and on, and people were born and grew up, and married, and died, and still all was summer and sleep and silence in the palace in the wood.

And at long last the hundred years were all but accomplished. There remained but one day of all their many, many, many days.

And on that day a prince came riding through the town. He stopped in the market-place, and said:

"Where is the country palace of your king?"

"We have no king," a stout grazier answered him; "we're a free and happy Republic, we are."

"But you had a king once," said the Prince. "Where was his country palace?"

"I've heard Granfer tell it was out yonder," said the grazier, "beyond the wood that no man can pass."

So the Prince went on, and by asking his way of all the old people he met on the country road he came at last to the wood that no man could pass.

"It ain't no good, master," said an old shepherd, who could just remember hearing that there *was* a palace inside there; "you'll never get through. What's set you on finding out a place that's dead and gone, and clean forgot?"

"I dreamed," said the Prince, "three happy nights I dreamed that within your king's country palace I should find the light of my eyes and the desire of my heart."

"And what are they?" the shepherd asked.

"I do not know yet," said the Prince, "but I shall know."

"I'd turn back and get me home along, if I was you," said the shepherd. "Why, suppose it was lions inside there, or dragons? There'd be a pretty how-de-do!"

"I can't turn back," said the Prince; "my dream is calling me, and I must follow. You take my horse and be good to him. If I come back safe to my own kingdom, I will pay you. If not, then you have a good horse for your pains."

So saying, he dismounted, drew his sword, and went forward to the wood.

"*You'll* never get through," said the old shepherd. "A many's tried that. Why, the boys is always at it. They never gets nothing but scratched faces and torn hands to show for it. What do *you* expect to get?"

"I don't know," said the Prince again; "but I *shall* know."

And he struck with his sword at the great twisted branches interwoven with briars and thick honeysuckle and thorny eglantine. And though they were so hard and thorny, at the touch of his sword they grew soft as dandelion stalks, so that he cut his way through them as easily as a man mows young grass with a scythe.

"Well, if ever I did!" said the old shepherd.

The Prince went on deeper and deeper to find the heart of the wood, and when he found the heart it was a green garden, all bright and fair and orderly, with rolled grass plots and smooth paths, and roses of all the colours there are, and starry tangles of jasmine. And in the middle of the wood's heart was the palace of his dreams. The garden was so still that it seemed to him as though he might even yet be dreaming, so he plucked a red rose, and smelt it, and knew that it all was real, and no dream.

On he went, up the terraces and through the hall, where, at the table, and at their service, King, Queen and courtiers slept, looking like life-sized figures in wax. At the end of the hall were golden curtains, and it was from behind them that his dream beckoned to him. He parted the curtains and went in. There on the carved ebony bed lay the Princess, between the silver cloth curtains, covered with cloth of gold, and with the veil of white gauze laid over her from head to feet. He turned down the veil, and set his red rose beside the others that lay at her breast, fresh and dewy as when they had been plucked a hundred years ago.

"Waken," he said softly, "oh, waken! Light of my eyes! Desire of my heart!"

But the Princess did not awake. Then he put his hand on the silver cloth pillow, and leaned over and kissed her softly, and she put up her arm sleepily round his neck, and kissed him back.

Then she woke, and jumped up, throwing back the golden coverlet.

"Oh, is it you?" she cried. "What a long time you've been! I've been dreaming about you for a hundred years!"

Then they went out into the hall, hand in hand, to tell the King and Queen that they were engaged to be married. And of course the King and Queen were awake, and the courtiers. The page finished filling the cup, the butler set the fruit on the table; down at the kennels the huntsman went on feeding the hounds; the cat scratched herself and yawned; and the pigeons circled round the little turrets that were like pepper-pots.

"Mother dear," said Princess Benevola, running up to the Queen and whispering in her ear, "this is my dear Prince who came and woke me up—and I'm going to marry him, and we've never been introduced, and I don't even know his name!"

So they were married, and all the people in the country forgot their Republican dream, and woke up as loyal as ever, and all the bells were set a-ringing, and all the children scattered roses of all the colours there are for the bride to walk on as she came out of church.

And when Malevola heard of it she lay down and died of sheer spite to think that anyone in the world was so happy as the Prince, and his bride who had been for a hundred years the Sleeping Beauty in the wood!

THE WHITE CAT

THERE WAS ONCE a king who attended very thoroughly to all his duties, and took a great pleasure and interest in the business of kingship. He brought up his sons very carefully, and had them trained by the best masters, so that when he should be tired of the cares of state his sons should be able to take up the burden, and rule the land as wisely as their father had done. And everything turned out as he wished. When their education was completed they were three as promising princes as any Prime Minister could wish to do business with. The only drawback was that the King still wished to do business with his Prime Ministers himself. Children do grow up so quickly, and when the princes were of an age to become kings the King himself was not nearly so tired as he expected to be, and did not at all want to retire from trade. And his trade—kingship—was the only trade his sons had learned. And it is not good for anyone, even princes, not to work at some trade or other. The King knew this as well as you or I do; but he could not make up his mind to retire. So he called his sons into his counting-house one day, and said:

"My dear boys, you have worked very hard, and passed all your exams with the utmost brilliancy and distinction. I am very pleased with you."

"Thank you, sir," said all the princes, and waited to hear that their brilliancy and distinction were to be rewarded with a share in the government of the kingdom.

No such thing.

"You must all be very tired," said the King, "after working so hard all these years. You need a holiday. So I propose to make each of you a little present of a nice convenient castle, a thousand men-at-arms, and a duenna to receive your girl friends, so that you can have dances and banquets and festivities of all sorts. And here are ten sacks of gold for each of you. So now run away and play. Be good boys, and enjoy yourselves. Youth's the season for enjoyment, and the old man's good for a few more years yet."

The two elder sons, who in fairy tales are always much more silly than the youngest, were delighted. They thanked their father warmly; so did the youngest, because he was both polite and affectionate. Then they all retired from the presence, and the King breathed a sigh of relief, and, taking the royal pen from the royal ear, plunged once more into the joyous labyrinth of the royal accounts. Artemesius and Demetrius set off at once for their castles, and did exactly as their father had told them, enjoying themselves in every luxurious way possible to clever, handsome young men with more money than they could spend. But Hyacinth, the youngest son, did otherwise. He went to his castle, sent a large order to his bookseller, and divided his time between study, sport, and the management of his estates. He found out everything about all his tenants, reduced rents when they were too high, rethatched the labourers' cottages, rebuilt the barns and stables, saw to it that everyone on his land had work to do, and good wages for his work, so that in a short time everyone on his estate was busy and happy, and wherever he went he met only loving and contented faces.

Demetrius and Artemesius did not make their retainers contented. They were not even contented themselves. In spite of all the pleasures, they were always grumbling, and saying that it was time the old man gave up business and let them be kings. And of course there were plenty of ill-natured gossips to carry the news of their discontent to their father. There were good-natured gossips too, and they brought the tale of the youngest son's doings.

Then the King thought, "If I give up my kingdom and divide it among my three sons, two-thirds of it will be ill-governed and neglected"—he was always good at arithmetic, this king—"and I can't give the whole kingdom to Hyacinth, though I should like to, because if I did the other two would be really annoyed. Let me put on my considering cap."

He got it out of the drawer where it always lay, wrapped in tissue paper, so that the gold embroidery on it should not tarnish, put it on, and sat thinking till thinking grew into sleep. When he woke up he instantly wrote to his three boys to come home.

Of course they came. And when they had all had supper he said:

"My dear boys, it seems a pity to divide up a handsome kingdom like this. And unsportsmanlike. I should prefer to put all my money on one horse, as they say in circles in which I have not moved. Now, do you agree to this? The one who brings me the nicest little dog within a year shall have the kingdom, and the other two shall have the nice castles they've got already."

Hyacinth agreed, he was always ready to please his father. The other two agreed because each in his greedy heart wanted the whole kingdom, and hoped by this means to get it.

The two eldest went back to their castles, and paid men to travel into all the countries of the world looking for pretty little dogs. But Hyacinth went himself to look for the kind of little dog his father wanted. He did not find it. Instead he found himself lost in a dark wood on a rainy night. His horse, frightened by the sudden whirr of a cock pheasant, who was frightened too, bolted, and Hyacinth was swept from his saddle by the bough of a tree. Bruised, muddy, wet, breathless, and extremely uncomfortable, he heard his horse's hoofs splashing along the wet path, fainter and fainter, and perceived that, for the first time in his life, he was alone, with no friends, no servants, no horse, no map, and no matches. It was a dismal moment. But he did not lose courage.

"Well," he told himself, "if I keep on walking I shall certainly get somewhere"; and that, as you know, is usually the case with all of us, even if we are not princes. And it happened just as he expected. When he had been walking for three hours and three-quarters through the dripping-wet wood he saw a light, and, with the intelligence that marks the youngest son in fairy stories, made for it. It grew brighter and brighter, and presently he came out of the thick wood into a broad park-like place, and then he saw the light came from the many windows of a great building.

"If it's an inn," he told himself, "I can get a bed and a supper. If it's a king's palace I shall have a welcome, and luxury. If it's a lunatic asylum—which is what it looks like—what place more suited to a prince who lets his horse rub him off against the branches of trees? And if it's a museum they can't refuse me shelter as a natural curiosity—a prince who knows when he's made an idiot of himself!"

So he went on boldly.

The park ended in a great avenue of quiet trees; the avenue ended in a garden of dripping rose alleys, and the garden ended at a marble terrace, from which marble steps led up to a very grand front door. It was shut.

"What shall I do now?" Hyacinth asked himself. And himself answered with some common-sense, "Ring the front-door bell." So he did.

And immediately the front door opened; and before the Prince could say, "Please, is your master at home?" he saw that there was no ear there to hear him. There was no ear, but there were hands, twelve pairs of them, with little blue clouds at the part where the wrist turns into the arm in ordinary people. And, without saying a word—for they did not seem to know the deaf-and-dumb language—the hands caught hold of him, pulled him in, and shut the door.

"This is a magic castle," said Hyacinth, who was not without intelligence. "I've read of such things, of course, but I've never seen one. How interesting!"

The hands led him through the warm, softly lighted hall, into a bath-room, where they undressed him, just as they do the poor men who have to go into workhouses—only much more gently. They pushed him into the water, which was warm and scented, and filled a silver bath sunk below the level of the marble floor. And when he was warm and clean these kind hands fetched him clean, soft new clothes, which fitted perfectly, brushed his hair for him, gave him a clean pocket-handkerchief, and took him straight away into a beautiful banqueting hall, built of carved spar that glittered like diamonds in the light of a thousand candles. A little round table was laid ready for dinner.

"Now," said Hyacinth, "I shall see my host, the wicked magician." He was not afraid of wicked magicians, because he carried the only amulet that has power against them—a clear-as-crystal heart.

The hands put a chair for him, and pushed it in behind him so decidedly that he sat down with great suddenness. Then a door at the end of the hall, where the daïs was, opened suddenly, and a little person, about eighteen inches high, veiled in black lace, walked with slow dignity towards him. This little person was attended, not by courtiers or men-at-arms, but by cats, dressed as maids-of-honour or as cavaliers; and when it came close to him, and raised its veil, Hyacinth saw that it too was a cat—a beautiful blue-eyed, white cat.

He got up and bowed. It was the only thing he could think of. It would never have done, he felt, to stroke this cat, who was, from the manner of her courtiers, quite plainly the mistress of the house, or to call her "Poor pussy then!"

She returned his bow, and then, to his amazement, spoke.

"I am very pleased to see you," she said. "Do sit down, and we will have dinner."

"Thank you very much," said the Prince, trying to conceal his surprise. "It is very kind of you to make a stranger so welcome."

So they sat down and had dinner.

"This," said the White Cat, "is a dish of stewed field-mice, and this——"

"Oh, thank you so much," said the Prince hastily. "I don't know how it is—it's a curious thing, but somehow I'm not hungry."

"Did you really think," said the White Cat gently, "that I should feed you on mice? The second dish is roasted pigeons; and you may be quite sure that everything that is offered you at my table will be real Prince's food, not cat's food."

"I beg your pardon," said Hyacinth, in confusion. "I might have known."

When you have been waited on by armless hands, and have had a short conversation with a cat, nothing can surprise you much. All your surprisedness seems to be used up. So Hyacinth was hardly astonished at all to find, as dinner went on, that the White Cat had read all the books that he had read and more besides, that she loved good music, and had seen all the beautiful pictures in all the fine picture galleries of the world. Her conversation was wise and witty, and full of gentle fun; also she seemed to be one of those people who make you trust them, so that you tell them things that you never meant to tell anyone; and long before the evening was over Hyacinth had told her the whole story of his life, his hopes, his dreams, his ambitions, as well as the fact that he was just now on a journey looking for the smallest and handsomest dog in the world. And the cat said:

"Do you trust me?"

And Hyacinth said, "Yes," which was quite true.

And then the White Cat promised that if he would stay a year at her castle she would give him at the end of that time exactly the dog he wanted.

Then they talked again of all sorts of things, as people do whose minds are in accord, and when at last it was time to say good-night Hyacinth told himself that never in all his life had he spent so pleasant an evening.

The next morning brought clear blue sky, and the trees and grass that had been drenched in last night's rain sparkled and glistened in the fresh sunlight. Hyacinth awoke with the feeling that he had something very pleasant to look forward to. He laughed at himself when he remembered that what he was looking forward to was the companionship of a white cat!

The morning was spent in hunting. Hyacinth rode a clockwork horse, that carried him across country as gaily as any horse in the King's stables could have done, and the White Cat rode a big monkey. They had very good sport, and brought home plenty of game, both cat-game and prince-game. The evening passed in conversation and the music of an invisible orchestra, and the whole day seemed shorter than an hour. And as time went on the weeks were as short as days, and the months as short as weeks; and the year came to an end only too soon.

Every day the Prince discovered something fresh to like in the White Cat, and when at last only one day of the year was left he was so sad that after supper the White Cat asked him what was the matter.

"I don't want to leave you," said he.

"I don't want you to go," said she; "but you must come back to me."

"I shall live for nothing else," said the Prince.

"Here's your little dog," said the White Cat, and gave him a walnut. "The dog's inside. Listen; you can hear it bark."

He listened, and sure enough he did hear a very faint little far-away bark.

Then when he had thanked her she held out her white paws for goodbye, and he pressed them gently.

"Goodbye," she said, "and come back to me."

Next day he set out for his father's house—not on the clockwork horse, which people would certainly have laughed at, but on a big real charger, caparisoned in a manner proper to his condition.

"Now, then," said the King upon his throne, when all the courtiers were assembled and the three princes were standing together on the throne steps, "let's see these dogs of yours."

Artemesius pulled a little dog out of his breast pocket —a dog so small and so handsome that everyone thought there could not be one handsomer and smaller in all the world. And all the courtiers clapped and shouted.

"You wait a bit," said Demetrius, and pulled out a little box. It had cotton-wool in it, and nestling in the cotton-wool a dog smaller and handsomer by far than his brother's.

So every one clapped more than ever. "I'm afraid you're out of it this time, Hyacinth, my boy," said the King.

But Hyacinth said, "I think not, sir," pulled out his walnut, cracked it, and out jumped the tiniest and most beautiful little white dog that ever was. It jumped from Hyacinth's hand into the King's state-velvet lap, and when his Majesty took off his state signet-ring and held it up the little dog leaped through it like a harlequin through a paper hoop.

And the courtiers and everybody else cheered so that you could hear them ten miles off.

But the King said:

"You're all very good boys, and I'm very pleased with you. Now just run along, like dear fellows, and get me a piece of cloth so fine that it will go through the eye of a needle. Take time—I sha'n't expect you till a year is out; and meantime I'll be getting on with those nice new laws I'm just making about trade arbitration."

Very disappointed indeed, the elder brothers bowed and turned away. This new quest was a nuisance, but they cheered up, and reminded each other that anything was better than that Hyacinth should have the throne. So they sent out messengers to collect fine cloth, and went back to their castles to enjoy themselves in their own way.

But Hyacinth went back to his White Cat, and the year went by so quickly that it seemed it had only just begun when it was time to return to the King with the piece of cloth so fine that it could go through the eye of a needle. The year was spent in study, and good talk, with music and all sorts of pleasures, and when its end came it was much harder than before to part with the White Cat.

However, it had to be done. He kissed the White Cat on the top of her furry head, and with tears in his eyes said "Goodbye."

She gave him an acorn, inside which, she said, he would find the fine cloth.

"And come back to me, Hyacinth," she said, "come back once more—even if you win the kingdom."

"I shall live for nothing else," said the Prince, and rode away very sad indeed.

Once more the King sat on his throne with all his courtiers about him, and the brothers produced their pieces of cloth. Both were wonderfully fine, much finer than you would think possible, but neither of them would begin to go through the eye of a needle, though the keeper of the King's laundry did her best and used a number six darner.

Then Hyacinth took out his acorn, and said, "My piece of cloth is inside." Of course everyone laughed, because it seemed impossible. He cracked the acorn, and instead of finding the cloth he found only a beech nut. Everyone laughed louder, but he cracked the beech nut, only to find a cherry stone. Then indeed everyone laughed in good earnest, the brothers more than any one, and the King rocked himself upon his golden throne, with tears of laughter in his eyes. Hyacinth flushed scarlet, but he cracked the cherry stone with his teeth, and inside it was a grain of wheat.

"Oh, White Cat, my White Cat," he said in his heart, "is it possible that you have betrayed me?"

And he hesitated, with the wheat grain in his hand. Then he remembered her wise, green eyes, her soft, purring voice, her kindness and cleverness and fondness. He thought of her soft, velvety paws, and almost fancied he felt their touch on his hands.

"No," he thought, straightening himself and looking proudly round the hall, "she would never betray me."

So he took out his penknife and opened the wheat grain. Inside was a grain of millet; and by this time there was not a dry eye in the room, because everybody had laughed till they cried.

Hyacinth set his teeth. "I won't fail in faith," he said, and split the millet seed on the knife-edge. And then all the laughter stopped short as if it had been turned off by a tap. For out of the tiny split millet seed tumbled heaps on heaps and yards on yards of white cambric, an ell wide, and so fine that it passed easily through the eye of a number ten sewing needle.

There was a great silence in the Court. Then a shout went up that shook the old banners on the walls.

But the King did not shout. He only said, "Very nice—very nice indeed. I'm very pleased with you all, and in a year from now you must each bring me the loveliest princess you can find, and then I'll retire from business, and the one with the handsomest wife can have the throne."

So they had to pretend not to be disappointed, and went off to their castles—all but Hyacinth, who went to his White Cat.

She was more pleased than ever to see him, and the third year passed more quickly than even the first two had done. She promised to find him a beautiful princess at the end of the year; but when the year's end came he suddenly said to her, as they sat in the rose-garden where the sun-dial was:

"Oh, White Cat, my White Cat, what do I want with princesses? I only want you."

"Oh, but that's nonsense," said the White Cat.

"It's the only wisdom in the world," said Hyacinth. "You are wise and witty and kind, and very, very dear, and I can't part with you for any princess, however beautiful. Oh, if you were only a princess! It's only your cat shape that stands between us. Is there no magician in the world that can turn you into a princess for my sake—or else turn me into a cat for yours?"

The White Cat looked long at him with her beautiful green eyes.

Then she said, "Do you really mean it?"

"I mean nothing else," said he. "I care for nothing else but you. Is there no magician who can do this?"

"No one," said the White Cat, "can do it but you. If you care for me so much as you say, take out your sword, cut off my head and tail, and throw them into the fire."

"I'd rather die," said he.

"Then you don't really love me," said she. "Dear, it's the only way. You've trusted me before. Trust me this once again."

She led him into the great hall, where a fire burned always, winter and summer, and reached down his sword from the hook where it hung.

"Oh, my White Cat!" he said, "my dear, own White Cat!"

"Strike!" she said, and raised her furry head. "Have faith, and strike!"

So he had faith, and struck, and the round head rolled on the floor. And still he had faith, and struck off the long white tail, and picked up the head and the tail and threw both into the fire, and the flames licked the white fur to brown.

"Oh, my own White Cat," he said, "then this is the end of everything!" And the tears ran down his face so that he could not see.

But suddenly he felt kind arms round his neck, a soft face laid against his, and a voice spoke, and it was the voice of his own White Cat.

"My own Prince," she said, "look at me, and see how beautiful I am!"

And he looked, and she was indeed as beautiful as any dream, tall and fair and strong—a splendid Princess.

"I was changed into a white cat," she explained as well as she could, for his kisses and love-words, "by a wicked fairy, and doomed to keep that shape till some one loved me enough to trust me utterly. You have loved me enough for that, and we are going to be the happiest lovers in all the world."

There seemed to be no doubt of that.

Next day they journeyed to the Court of the King, followed by a long and glorious train of noble ladies and gallant knights and stalwart men-at-arms, and the procession was like a magnificent ribbon laid across the green country, so long it was, and so bright with silk and velvet and with gold and jewels. For the stroke of Hyacinth's sword had freed from enchantment not only the White Cat herself, but all her Court, who had been enchanted with her.

Demetrius and Artemesius had found two lovely princesses, but their beauty paled as starlight before sunshine in the presence of the beauty of the White Cat Princess.

"Well, Hyacinth, my boy," said the King, sighing heavily, "I suppose there's no getting out of it this time. I'm sure I hope you'll be very happy, my dears," he added forlornly.

Then the White Cat Princess rose up from the silver throne that had hastily been wheeled forward for her by the King's orders, and kneeled in front of the King, and said:

"Please, your Majesty and dear father-in-law, keep your kingdom and go on governing it. You do do it so nicely. I have three kingdoms of my own. Hyacinth and I will take one of them, and the other two we will give to Demetrius and Artemesius, as soon as your Majesty is satisfied that they have learned on their own estates the way to rule wisely."

And she smiled so kindly and gently at the elder princes that they were not angry or ashamed at her words, only grateful for her splendid present. And the courtiers shouted till you could have heard them twenty miles off; and they cleared away the chairs and tables, and thrones, and carpets and things, and had a dance then and there, because every one was so happy.

"You know, my dear," said the old King, mopping his forehead and putting his crown straight after leading off with the White Cat Princess in the first country dance, "you know I really *do* think it's best for me to go on being King. It's the only business I really understand, and I couldn't learn another trade so late in life, and I never could bear to be idle."

"Exactly," said she; "so now everybody's pleased."

And, so beyond doubt, everybody was.

HOP-O'-MY-THUMB

IN A VERY small hut beside a very big forest there once lived a poor man whose only way of getting a living was to pick up sticks, tie them in bundles, and carry them to the town, where he sold them. He managed in this way to make just enough to keep himself and his wife, but not enough to keep his family. He had seven children, all boys, and none of them ever had quite enough to eat. The father's spirit had been broken by long poverty, or he would certainly have cut a purse on the high-road or robbed a till rather than do the dreadful thing which in the end he did. As for his wife, she must have been an idiot, or worse.

This poor man used to look at his children as they sat round the table eating at one meal the bread that would have kept him and his wife for three days, and by degrees the idea got into his head that if he could only get rid of his seven children he and his wife would have enough to eat, which at present they never did have. And one night when the children had gone to bed in the cock-loft that served for a dormitory, he leaned his elbows on the table, and his head in his hands, and said:

"Wife, our children are starving, and so are we. I can't bear to see them die of starvation—now don't contradict me, because I won't stand it. If you can bear it, I can't. Tomorrow I shall take them into the forest and lose them there. Perhaps some rich man may find them—such things have happened. Anyway, you and I will get enough to eat when they are gone."

"Never," said his wife. "How can you dare to think of doing such a wicked thing? Take *me* out and lose *me* in the forest. I don't mind starving or being eaten by wolves, but I won't have it done to my babies, so I tell you."

And she began to cry—very loudly, and very miserably.

"Hold your noise," said the father, "and listen to me. If we keep the children here we shall starve together. But if I take them into the forest they're not at all certain to be eaten by wolves. The King might come riding by, and adopt the lot of them; or some richer woodcutter than I might take them as servants; or they might find a pot of gold. Anyhow, tomorrow morning I'm going to take them out and lose them; and if you dare to interfere I'll kill you first, and then I'll kill the children, and then I'll kill myself, and the matter will be settled once for all."

So the mother, being, as I said, a very silly woman, said, "Very well, I see it's the best thing we can do." And then they talked over their horrible plan for a while, and at last raked the ashes together, to keep the fire alive for next day, and went to bed.

Now someone had been listening at the key-hole, and this someone was Hop-o'-my-Thumb. He was the youngest of the seven children, and when he was born he was only as long as his father's thumb, so they gave him that name. And he was a very silent child, who hardly ever spoke, but he listened to everything. His brothers used to make fun of him, and call him "Silly Billy," and he had to do most of the housework, that ought to have been done by all seven—share and share alike.

Now when Hop-o'-my-Thumb woke up and heard his mother crying he crept out of bed, and, as I said, he listened at the door, which is considered a very dishonourable thing to do, except in case of war. But I suppose if you happen to have a father and mother like that faggot-maker and his wife it is quite as dangerous as war, and you have to act accordingly.

Hop-o'-my-Thumb heard all their plans, and he thought and thought. Being such a silent child, he had had a good deal of practice in thinking, and he did it rather well. When he thought he had thought enough, he curled up in the ragged blanket and went to sleep.

Next morning the children went down to the brook to wash their hands and faces, and Hop-o'-my-Thumb filled all his pockets with small white stones from the brook's edge, and when his father said, "Come, children, let's go into the forest, and I'll show you how to set a snare for bears," and all the children eagerly followed, Hop-o'-my-Thumb lagged behind, and every ten paces he dropped a white stone, so that the road should be marked by them, and he should be able to find his way back again. The father led them by ways they did not know, and he turned this way and he turned that way, till none of the boys knew even in which direction their home lay, much less the way to get to it.

Then this odd sort of father set the children to dig a pit to trap bears in, and when the poor little dears were working their hardest, and thinking how pleased he would be to see them so industrious, he just slipped away and left them, and went hurrying back to his wife, to tell her he had succeeded in losing their seven sons, and now there would be enough for father and mother to eat. I am glad the fathers and mothers that we have now are not like that.

When the seven children had dug as much as they could, they stopped digging—which was bound to happen—and then they found that they were lost in the wood, or rather their father was lost, for they could not find him. And of course that came to the same thing. They all began to cry, except Hop-o'-my-Thumb; and little Robin, who was his mother's blue-eyed darling, cried more and louder than any of the others.

Then Hop-o'-my-Thumb put his legs very far apart, and stuck his hands on his hips, and looked as manly as he could, and "Cry-babies!" said he.

"Cry-baby yourself," said his eldest brother.

"I'm not," said Hop-o'-my-Thumb. "You just look at me. My face is as dry as a bone. For why? I know how to find the way home, and you don't. And if you call me names I'll go home by myself, and leave you here in the forest. *Cry-baby!*"

So saying, he turned and walked away; and the others followed him, because there seemed nothing else to do.

He led the way to the place where he had dropped the last of the white stones. "Now," he said, "keep your eyes open, for by these white stones we shall find our way home. And keep your mouths shut when you get there, for we may have to do this little trick again."

Now when the wood-cutter got back from the forest after getting rid of his children he was met at the door by a servant who had come on horseback from the King to pay eight crowns that had been owing for firewood. So now there was money to get things to eat, and he sent his wife down to the village to buy food. And she did; and when she had cooked supper they sat down to eat it; and it was not till they had satisfied their hunger that the mother began to cry because the children were not there to clear up the dish. The children by this time had found their way home, and were listening outside the door, and when they heard their mother say, "I wish the dear children were here to share this supper with us," they rushed in, and their father and mother were really glad to see them.

But the eight silver crowns were presently spent, and the family as poor as ever. And again the father decided to lose the children, and again Hop-o'-my-Thumb overheard their cruel plans. He was not much troubled. He felt that he could get out of the forest as before, by laying a track of white pebbles. But he reckoned without that little sneak and mother's darling, Robin, who had told all about the pebbles; so that when Hop-o'-my-Thumb got up early to fill his pockets he found the door locked.

"Never mind," he said to himself; "I won't eat my breakfast, and I'll crumble the bread—the crumbs will do
instead of pebbles to mark the way home."

But alas! when everything had happened as before, and
when he started to lead his brothers proudly home, he
could not do it. For the crumbs were gone. The birds had
eaten them.

"Never mind," said Hop-o'-my-Thumb; "let us just walk
towards the sun. We shall get out of the wood some time,
and we'll go to the first house we see and ask for a night's
lodging. Perhaps they'll take us on as servants. I know
how to work, and if the rest of you don't, you ought to."

None of the others could think of any better plan, so
they followed Hop-o'-my-Thumb towards the setting sun.
And they walked, and they walked, and they walked, and
they walked, and everyone was tired out, even the sun,
which had gone to bed, before they came to a big house
with spiky iron railings. A light shone through a round
window over the porch, and there was a big knocker to
the door—too high for them to reach. But the eldest boy
made a back, and Hop-o'-my-Thumb got on it, and knocked
loudly.

A kind-looking old lady opened the door.

"Sakes alive!" she said, looking down at the seven tired
little boys. "What do *you* want at this time of night?"

Hop-o'-my-Thumb said, "A night's lodging and a bit of
bread, your Majesty."

The lady laughed a jolly laugh.

"Bless you," she said, "I'm not the Queen! I'm Mrs.
Gruffky, and my husband is an ogre, I am sorry to say, and
eats little children. So you'd best be off the way you came,
before he catches you. Go on to the next house. It's only
four miles away."

"We can't," said Hop-o'-my-Thumb. "We're too tired to
go on for forty yards, let alone four miles. Hide us for the
night, good lady, and give us a crust, and we'll go on early
in the morning."

The other six began to cry, and the ogre's wife was so sorry for them that she said, "Well, come in, if you must. But don't blame me if anything goes wrong."

With that she opened the door wide, and they followed her into the big warm kitchen, where a whole sheep was roasting before the fire for the ogre's supper. She let the children warm themselves, and gave them bread and hot dripping with salt on it, which is called sop-in-the-pan, and is much nicer than you would think.

They soon felt very comfortable and jolly, and quite forgot their tiredness and all their misfortunes. And then suddenly there was a great knocking at the door, and it was the ogre come home.

"Quick, quick! Hide! Here he comes!" whispered Mrs. Gruffky, and pushed the seven boys behind the red window-curtains.

"Is supper ready?" said the ogre; "and have you drawn my bucket of red wine?"

"Oh, yes," said his wife, "it's all ready, and I'll dish up at once."

Soon the whole sheep was smoking in a dish, and the ogre sat down to supper. But he had not eaten more than two or three of the joints when he began to sniff.

"What's this I smell?" he said. "Young flesh—live flesh—child's flesh?"

"Perhaps," said his wife, "it is the sucking-pigs that are hanging in the dairy ready for your breakfast."

"No, no, it's boys' flesh," said the ogre; "you don't deceive me so easily." He got up and looked about. The red curtains shook with the trembling of the children. The ogre saw the movement, pulled back the curtains, and caught up the boys, four in one hand and three in the other.

"There's a nice trick to play on a man," he said, and put them in the kneading-trough. Then he sharpened his knife.

"They'll make a savoury pie," he said. "I'll kill them at once, and they'll be tender eating tomorrow."

"Nonsense!" said his wife. "Think of all the meat we've got in the house. How can you be so wasteful? There's more than half that sheep, and a large calf in the larder, and a bullock, and those sucking-pigs. And I ordered three hogs to be killed this morning, which will be brought in tomorrow. Let us keep the children and fatten them up a bit. See how thin they are. That's why I hid them. I meant them for a little surprise for you. I know how impatient you always are. Let me put them to bed. In a day or two they'll be really nice eating."

"Very well," said the ogre. "Feed the little wretches and put them to bed."

So she did. She hoped to save their lives by this delay. But the ogre could not sleep for thinking of that raised pie, and when his wife had gone to sleep he got up quietly, and went down and sharpened his knife on the hearthstone.

The ogre's wife had put all the children to sleep in one big bed, and she had found little night-gowns and nightcaps for them. In another bed in the same room were the ogre's seven daughters, who all slept with gold crowns on their heads. Soon everyone in that room was sleeping, except Hop-o'-my-Thumb, who had his wits about him. He got up as quietly as the ogre was doing, and, taking the crowns off the seven girls, he put them on his own and his brothers' heads. And he put the seven little cotton nightcaps on the heads of the ogre's daughters. And it was just as well that he did.

For when the ogre had finished sharpening his knife he came upstairs, in the dark, for he could not find the tinder-box. He came straight to the bed where the boys lay, and, feeling in the dark, his hand found the gold crowns.

"Dads-lads!" he said, "I had like to have made a pretty mistake here." Then he went to the next bed, and felt the cotton night-caps.

"No mistake this time," said he, and cut seven throats, so that every one in that bed died without moving. And

the ogre went back to bed thinking how clever he had
been.

When Hop-o'-my-Thumb knew that the ogre was
asleep—it was quite easy to know, for his snores shook
the house and made the doors and windows rattle—he
woke his brothers, and they dressed in the dark—all but
their boots, which they carried in their hands. They
crept down the stairs—their hearts in their mouths at
every creak of the old boards—got into the silent, warm
kitchen, and then through a window into the night. Then
they ran as hard as they could—not much caring where
they ran, so long as it was away from that dreadful
house.

When the ogre found out the mistake he had made, and
that he had killed his own daughters, he was very angry.
He called for his seven-league boots, and set out to find
the children. He strode here and there, over mountains
and rivers, taking twenty-one miles at every step, and
looking high and low for Hop-o'-my-Thumb and his brothers.

When they saw him striding about in this way they were
more frightened than ever, for he was taking such long
steps, and no one could tell in what direction the next
would be. So they hid in a cave by the river, and Hop-o'-
my-Thumb stood near the entrance, and peeped out to
see where the ogre was.

The ogre came close to the cave, and sat down outside.
He smelt his prey, but he did not hurry now to find it.

"They are hiding somewhere near here," he said, "and
when they move I shall nab them."

So he pulled off his boots to rest his feet, and presently
he fell fast asleep. Then Hop-o'-my-Thumb whispered to
his brothers to run softly and swiftly home, and he went
out to take the boots away and hide them. Now the boots
were, of course, fairy boots, and they were always the
right size for the person who had hold of them, so that
when Hop-o'-my-Thumb took hold of them to drag them

away they instantly shrank till they were a fine fit for his own little legs.

His first idea was to go and tell the King about the ogre, and to get the army to come and kill him, and he set out for the city; but before he had gone eighty-four miles (or four steps) one of the fairies of the boots spoke, and said, "Stop!"

So Hop-o'-my-Thumb stopped—though he could not think where the voice came from.

"I am the eldest fairy of the boots," the voice went on. "You are a good boy, and a brave boy, and a clever boy. You can get a fortune for your parents now, if you have the wit to do it. Never mind revenging yourself on the ogre. His fate is creeping towards him even now, rustling and evil, among the dried grass and hot stones of the riverside. Feel in your pocket, and crack the largest nut you find there."

He felt, and sure enough there was a pocketful of nuts where a moment ago no nuts had been. He cracked the largest with his teeth, and the teeth met on a paper. It was red, and on it in silver letters were these words:

> *"Hie thee to the ogre's door,*
> *These words whisper, nothing more:*
> *'Ogress, ogre cannot come;*
> *Big keys give to Hop-o'-my-Thumb.'"*

So he went to the ogre's house, and when the ogress opened the door he simply said the words the red paper had told him to say.

"Oh, la!" said the ogre's wife, "that means he's been caught at last, and wants a ransom. Is that so?"

"I am not to say anything more," said Hop-o'-my-Thumb.

"But why did he send you—you who were the cause of my daughters' deaths?"

"I mustn't say any more," said the boy, and repeated his lesson.

"Ogress, ogre cannot come;
Big keys give to Hop-o'-my-Thumb."

"Oh, well, here they are," she said, and reached them down from the nail. "Come to the treasure chamber. I'll have a pack-horse got ready to carry what you want. And be sure you take enough."

She led him to a room with thick stone walls and narrow windows, and there were jewels and money, and treasure of all sorts—enough to keep hundreds of poor families in luxury all their lives. This was the treasure the ogre had heaped up by robbing everyone he came across.

Hop-o'-my-Thumb took as much as he wanted, and the ogre's wife helped him to arrange it on the pack-horse, and he said goodbye to her, and went straight home to his father and mother, and gave it all to them. And I think it was very kind and forgiving of him. He himself went and laid his wits and his seven-league boots at the service of the King, who at once gave him the highest military honours, and dubbed him "General Post Office" on the spot.

The ogre was killed by a viper as he lay asleep outside that cave, and all the army turned out and dug a trench to bury him in.

The ogre's wife inherited all the rest of his wealth, and because she had been kind to him and his brothers Hop-o'-my-Thumb persuaded the King to honour her with the title of "Duchess of Draggletail".

The father and mother, now that they were no longer afraid of starving, were very sorry for the way they had treated their boys, and never again did anything that was not good and kind. Indeed, it was their poverty that was to blame more than they; for, after all, though wickedness sometimes makes people poor, yet much more often poverty makes them wicked. Which is not a bad thing to remember when we are judging our neighbours.